7/58

F
BAR

Barth, Richard,
1943-

Deadly climate

080665

$14.95

DATE			

D0961266

CUP
RLIN ★

DEADLY CLIMATE

...

DEADLY CLIMATE

...

RICHARD BARTH

...

ST. MARTIN'S PRESS

New York

Design by Robert Bull Design

14.95 88B4327

Library of Congress Cataloging-in-Publication Data
Barth, Richard, 1943-
   Deadly climate / by Richard Barth.
        p.   cm.
   ISBN 0-312-01756-1
   I. Title.
PS3552.A755D4 1988   87-38274
813'.54—dc 19   CIP

First Edition

10 9 8 7 6 5 4 3 2 1

Dedicated in Loving Memory to
SHIRLEY AND DAVID KLEINMAN

PROLOGUE

...

It had taken the thirty-three-foot Donzi only three hours to make the run in from Nassau. Even though the night was dark and moonless, the boat with its 330 Mercruisers kept to well over sixty knots until it hit the twelve mile limit and the stalking grounds of the United States Coast Guard and Customs Service. Then it throttled back to a less suspicious fifteen knots and made directly for the coordinates of Government Cut, the opening into Miami harbor.

On board were the two men who had rented the boat the day before from a marina in Fort Lauderdale. They were experts at boat-handling and maintenance, since each had spent several seasons on the South American racing circuit. The circuit paid well only if they won races. Delivering drugs paid well all the time.

In their possession this October evening were four kilos of uncut Colombian cocaine. It had come to them at the end of a long trail in the back tool shed of a seedy garage in Nassau. This was their fourth run in for their employer, whose name they didn't know but whose instructions had always been letter clear. In another half hour they'd make delivery, return the rented Donzi, then work their way back to the Miami area. Two days later they'd pick up their commission from a bus locker over on Flagler, then wait for the next call.

As the Donzi moved in toward the coastline, the driver checked the boat's own radar. Out here there wasn't much to worry about. If the Feds came out they'd be spotted soon enough and the two smugglers could double back for another try in a couple of days. The Donzi was faster than just about anything the Customs Service had and their drivers hadn't been honed on some of the tactics of South American coastal racing. The driver had scars across his chest from when he'd flipped a boat trying to do a 120-degree turn at fifty miles an hour, and that was only for a silver trophy and a few thousand dollars. Both men knew that their real worries would come inside Government Cut when there was no way for them to get back to the open ocean.

The radar was clear so the driver tapped the throttle down a quarter of an inch and rode the needle up to twenty knots. In the distance the two men could see the glow of Miami's lights in the low clouds. He motioned to his partner and the other man went to prepare the package for the drop-off.

On the floor just in front of the transom was a square plastic waterproof container about the size of a gallon of milk. The man bent over and zipped it into a special rubber bag with rigid circular handles. Through the handles he placed a commercial gaffing hook at the end of a five-foot pole. He checked that everything was secure, then walked back up to the driver.

"Twenty more minutes," the man at the controls said. "No one's out tonight. We won't have a problem."

■ ■ ■

The Customs Service boat was lying concealed behind Fisher Island just inside Government Cut. They had been monitoring the late night traffic going through both Government Cut and Norris Cut to the south. They had also been watching the radar reports coming in from their central processing station on the mainland. They were, in particular, curious about one sighting coming in from the direction of Nassau and still five or six miles out. It had the classic profile, a hot approach up to twelve miles, then a slowdown to blend in with coastal traffic. Their own twin 200-horsepower engines were idling softly, but as was usual they called in for a backup boat to move over to the south side of Lummus Island. Between the two of them, there was little chance a boat could get away once inside the bay. The men on board checked their weapons and waited. Fifteen minutes they figured, ten if the smugglers got impatient. Either way, they'd be ready.

■ ■ ■

Government Cut looked peaceful as the two South Americans motored through. To their right they saw the dark construction site of a new condominium complex going up in the South Beach, the skeletons of the tall buildings looking like children's toys against the backlighting of the Collins Avenue strip. Straight ahead was the port of Miami with its commercial docks and seaplane anchorage. The only things in between were the rest of Fisher Island, which made up the south side of the cut, and tiny Lummus Island.

A spot appeared on the Donzi's radar to port and the driver immediately raised his head to check it out. A little twenty-seven foot Catalina sailboat glided by fifty feet away under inboard power. The driver eased his tight grip on the wheel. Every few seconds now he scanned the radar as a double check. A minute later they were through the cut and angled to the right into Meloy channel.

It may have been the speed of the blip on the radar, or some sixth sense, but the driver of the Donzi slammed down the throttle almost before the sound of the approaching motor reached his ears. The Customs Service boat had bided its time and was now in behind them, severing their escape to the sea. Off to port the driver heard another powerful motor and in an instant realized he was in a trap. By then the Donzi was up to forty-five knots and accelerating. There was only one way to go; forward up the bay side of the beach. There was a chance he could outrun them into the canal and still make the drop. All he needed was a ten-second spot and they'd be clear. He wasn't worried about the boat coming in from Lummus. That one was farther away and had to swing around little Causeway Terminal Island to catch up. The problem was the boat to their rear no more than 200 yards back. He hoped its driver wasn't as crazy a son of a bitch as he was.

The Donzi flashed by the Flagler Memorial Monument at sixty knots and did a turn to port that strained every seam on the boat. They barely made the southern end of Di-Lido Island before the driver yanked the wheel hard right and took it into a gut-wrenching turn the other way. At that speed they just cleared through the second of the six Venetian Islands, skidding sideways with their starboard toe rail almost under water. Coming out on the other side of the causeway, they straightened out, just buzzed over the submerged edge of Pelican Island coughing up mud all the while from their straining propeller, and shot straight toward the northern opening of the Sunset Isles canal system. The driver looked over his shoulder and grinned. The maneuver seemed to have worked. He counted to twelve before he spotted the government boat behind him, now all lit up with enough flashing green, red and amber lights to qualify for the Orange Bowl parade. He had his margin.

When the captain of the pursuing boat saw his quarry heading straight for the little Sunset Islands he directed the second boat, perhaps a quarter mile behind him, to cover the southern outlet. Then he followed the smugglers' boat in, throttling back at the last possible minute. When they got into the narrow canal, the entire landscape was dancing from the wake of the first boat. Scores of small and large craft of every type were hammering off their moorings as waves continued to splash over bulkheads. They didn't catch up with the Donzi until they were around the gradual curve and had arrived at the canal's southern outlet, now blocked by their sister boat. The two men on the Donzi, trapped between the two police boats, cut the ignition and drifted with their forward momentum. They looked up at the eight rifles as well as two searchlights trained on them and grinned sheepishly. They had that luxury because they were absolutely clean, there wasn't a gram of any illegal substance or suspect paraphernalia on board, and their papers were in perfect order.

"What's the problem?" the driver asked with unveiled sarcasm. "Was I speeding?"

CHAPTER 1

...

It was the craziest thing she'd done all month. After carefully figuring the week's groceries at Sloan's, estimating the Con Ed take, factoring in the long distance call she'd made to her nephew in New Jersey, she wound up with a shortfall for the month of $14.34. Unlike the fiscal luminaries in the United States government, Margaret Binton didn't much believe in deficit spending or supply side economics, not for a seventy-two-year-old widow in New York City. It was, then, nothing short of madness when she dipped into her battered but serviceable old Kadin handbag and fished out the five-dollar bill. One of those incomprehensible moments in life when some outside force directed her actions without the slightest appeal to logic. She simply held out the banknote to her friend Berdie and waited for her receipt.

"Oh Margaret, I know you're going to win. Only a thousand raffle books were printed—twenty-five-thousand tickets. Much better odds than the lottery."

"I don't expect it really matters," Margaret said. "I haven't given anything all year to the church."

"And look at all you can win . . . transistor radios, toaster ovens, there's even some of those five-inch portable TV sets. Think how nice it would be to watch one of our favorite programs right here on the bench."

Margaret studied the receipt Berdie finally handed over.

"What's this picture of a bus for? One of the prizes a trip to Atlantic City?"

"That's no bus, that's the grand prize." Berdie pointed

6

excitedly. "A twenty-five-foot Winnebago deluxe recreational vehicle." She leaned back into the bench and raised her voice to overcome the noise of a passing truck on Broadway. "Sleeps four easy. It's got a kitchen, bathroom, dining area, good closet space. It's sitting right outside the church."

"Shuffleboard court on the roof?"

"What?" Berdie leaned closer. In the few years since she turned seventy, she'd started missing words. Nothing serious, an odd one here and there. Mostly she disregarded the blank spaces, unless it was a question. If anything, Berdie was always polite, except of course to Sid Rossman.

"Nothing." Margaret opened her bag again and took out the nearly empty pack of Camels. Damn, she thought, $19.34 down and I forgot about the cigarettes. She looked ruefully at the five-dollar bill her friend was now stuffing into the envelope with the other raffle books. "I suppose it's for a good cause." She shook out one of the remaining cigarettes and lit it. "Now where do you suppose I got this?" She showed Berdie the book of matches. On the cover in formal gold letters was the inscription Samuel Speigel, Bar Mitzvah, Plaza Hotel, October 31, 1979.

"Rose, more than likely. You're always bumming matches off her."

Margaret smiled lightly as she thought about Rose, the friendliest bag lady north of Times Square.

"In that case, I'm lucky they still work. Most of her matches have seen several puddles or snowbanks."

"You want to take a look at the Winnebago? It's only a few blocks."

"You serious?" Margaret inhaled deeply. "I can fantasize about a transistor . . . maybe stretch it into one of those small TVs, but I wouldn't even begin to know how to dream about an RV. No, it's more fun sitting here. Sun's out and Sid'll be along any minute." She winked. "If he had a good day at OTB yesterday he might be agreeable to a little loan. Lord knows I could use it.

Berdie stuffed the envelope into her Bloomingdale's shopping bag and shifted her attention to the dozen or so pigeons that were pecking to and fro around the bench. The crumbs she had spread twenty minutes before had long since been eaten and many of the savvier birds had already moved on to other Broadway locations. The neighborhood was crawling with scores of bird lovers who found daily contentment watching the hapless birds gorge themselves on stale bagel chips and leftover bread. If you were a pigeon in Manhattan and didn't hit Broadway around noon, you might just as well hang it up. But now, the few birds that remained were either extraordinarily lazy or too brain-damaged to notice the difference between morsels of genuine New York schist and Zabar's whole wheat. It made no difference. Berdie loved them all.

"I took a ticket myself," she announced reluctantly. "It was a hard decision, you know, choosing between my birds and who knows what . . . maybe a little radio, maybe nothing."

"You shouldn't feel guilty. Their little systems don't absolutely need your oregano-flavored bread crumbs. I think they'd be quite happy with stale bread."

"Perhaps." Berdie smoothed the cotton dress across her lap and looked up into the sky. "They are quite fragile though."

The two women sat quietly for a moment as the light changed on Broadway. A pack of pedestrians crossed in front of them, and one of the young boys, obviously a private school kid from the looks of his blue blazer, made a halfhearted karate kick at a nearby pigeon. Without hesitation, Berdie jumped up, raised her shopping bag, and chased him off the island. When she returned, Sid was sitting in her place. He had a broad smile on his face, an expression of friendly sarcasm.

"Defending the rights of the defenseless again?"

"Buzz off," she shot back. "You're in my seat."

"A public bench," Sid said and opened his copy of the *Racing Form*. He then reached into what at one time had been a fairly natty houndstooth jacket and removed a stubby pencil. From twenty feet away he could have been Leonard Bernstein poring over a new score. Neatly groomed silver hair, intelligent concentrated expression, the same square athletic build. Except of course he wasn't Bernstein and the only music he liked to hear was the call of the horses to the track. He waited just long enough to insure he had Berdie's pressure up before he started in on the birds.

"Too bad the kid missed. Another couple inches and he would'a put the poor thing out of his misery. Fact is," Sid continued without looking up, "they make damn good targets."

Berdie clenched her bag tighter, took a deep breath, then with obvious effort, came out with the most benign smile.

"If, Mr. Rossman, you are trying to get a rise out of me, it won't work. Not today." She bent down and grabbed a book of raffle tickets. "I am going to get something out of you."

"Saint Ignatius? I'm afraid to disappoint you, Berdie, but Pancher got to me yesterday. To coin a phrase, I already gave at the office. He was lucky enough to catch me after a win in the third."

She sighed and put the book back. "Damn, I got two more books." She looked past Sid at Margaret. "You got any ideas?"

"The Florence E. Bliss Senior Center?"

Berdie shook her head. "Did it."

"Grossman's Bakery on Eighty-eighth?"

"For a church raffle . . ."

Margaret crushed out the cigarette. "What about the Eighty-second precinct. Maybe Morley or Schaeffer would do you a favor. We've certainly done them enough."

Berdie brightened. "That's an idea. Why didn't I think of it?"

"Probably," Sid said, "because cops are in the business of selling raffles, not buying them." He closed his paper and leaned back. "And you gotta believe in the basic even-handedness of lady luck. Cops are too cynical."

Margaret laughed. "But not you?"

"Are you kidding. I already kissed that money good-bye. It would'a done more good riding on something in the fourth. Hell, no one ever wins those things. Least of all, no one I ever knew."

CHAPTER 2

...

Six days later, at precisely 4:15 in the afternoon, Sid could no longer say that. Of course the good news hit the streets immediately but by then most of the benches were empty. It was a cold, blustery November day, the kind that Central Park West doormen hate. Scores of moist leaves went skittering through their immaculate marble lobbies and had to be chased down one by one before some litigious tenant took a swan dive.

Margaret's doorman faced no such dilemma. Her building's lobby on West Eighty-second Street had faded walls, a peeling ceiling, and plain linoleum floors leading to a tired old self-service elevator. If Harry Cohen got up four times during a shift, two of them were to relieve himself from the diuretic effects of his two earlier coffee breaks. He was a doorman only because no one had come up with the word yet for what Harry was best at: sitting cantilevered on his chair absorbed in a newspaper, somehow raising his head slightly at just the right moment to greet a tenant. Harry the nodman perhaps. When Berdie pushed her way into the lobby, Harry even added a few words.

"She's in, Mrs. Mangione. 'Bout twenty minutes."

"Harry, she won, she won!" and with that Berdie fairly skipped into the elevator. Harry watched the steel door close on the tiny cubicle and went back to Dick Young's problems with the Knick defense. He didn't give Berdie's utterance another thought until the front door opened again and Sid breezed in. This time Harry actually raised his head level.

"You too?"

"Does she know?"

"What the hell. I suppose so. Her friend Mangione just went up. You want to tell me what she won?"

"Everything, Harry. Everything." And in a second Sid was also inside the tiny elevator. This time Harry didn't go back to his paper. He sat motionless for a few minutes until he had it figured. Had to be the lottery. "Good lord." He brought his chair upright. "And she owes me twenty dollars."

■ ■ ■

From the confused expression on her face when she opened the door, it was obvious Margaret knew. Also, Berdie was standing behind her with a smile broad enough to subdue the Mormon Tabernacle choir. Sid looked from one to another and took a step inside.

"So what do you think?" he asked. "California, New Orleans . . ."

"I think it's insane," is what Margaret said. "I can hardly buy a pack of cigarettes, and now I have to come up with thousands of dollars in tax. Why couldn't it have just been one of the TVs?"

"But that's got to be a forty-thousand-dollar motor home, a retired person's dream," Berdie said incredulously.

"Not this retired person's. I think I'm going to say it's some big mistake, that I was only buying a ticket for the little things?"

Sid walked into the small, neat living room and sat down. "Something's not clicking here. You just won a recreation vehicle worth forty grand and you're going to disclaim it? I don't believe this. You got any scotch?"

Margaret shook her head. "Just some sherry in the kitchen."

Sid gave a pained expression and stayed where he was.

"What's not to believe?" Margaret continued. "You got the ten thousand to give Uncle Sam?"

"You'll get it," Berdie said innocently. "You'll figure something out. Maybe you can sell it."

"Right," Margaret chuckled. "I'm seventy-two years old and I have a whole lot of experience selling motor homes. Maybe I'll advertise it in the co-op section of the *Times*. 'One room, kitchen, bathroom, city views . . .'" she hesitated, "'possible country views.'" She came over and sat down in one of her easy chairs, the one under the oil painting of a bowl of fruit. It had been one of her late husband Oscar's favorites even though the artist had unwittingly captured the way fruit looks after three weeks in the South Texas sun.

There was a knock on the door at the precise moment Margaret kicked off her Dr. Scholls.

"That'll be Durso," Sid said. "I saw him at Saint Ignatius too."

Berdie saved Margaret the trouble of getting up. She opened the door and motioned with her head to come in. The newcomer took a step over the threshold and there could be no doubt that Sid had been correct. The odor of Edgeworth pipe tobacco preceded him by a good ten feet, and this, strangely, when he wasn't smoking it. After fifty years of loyalty to one brand, Durso's clothes, his eyeglasses, even his beret exuded Edgeworth. Mention the fact to him and he would have been dumbfounded.

"Congratulations, Margaret" was the first thing he said. "So where are we going with it?"

"I can see there is some deep misunderstanding here,"

Margaret countered. "I will try once again to clarify things." She looked slowly from one friend to another. "No RV."

The three of them exploded at once, but when the noise had died down, it was Durso who took the floor. Being a retired school teacher, he brought a certain authority to his delivery.

"Margaret," he began, "you are missing the obvious. I admit selling an RV on Broadway might be awkward, but selling it in Florida is as natural as fresh squeezed orange juice. The way I understand it, there are more RVs on the roads down there than cars. People like us moving about, west coast, east coast, down to the Keys. It would be no problem to drive right in to a dealer and unload it for a nice piece of change. Certainly enough to pay the tax and then some."

"And you'd get a free trip out of it," Sid added. "You've always been talking about your dream trip. Take as long as you like . . . no worries, you got your own free accommodations."

"And you needn't be alone," Berdie prompted. "I'm sure you could find some friends to travel with."

"No doubt," Margaret said.

"Just take a look," Berdie continued. "Before you do something rash, the thing is sitting right outside Saint Ignatius. The keys are waiting at the desk."

Durso opened the newspaper and after a moment found what he was looking for. "Eighty-four and sunny yesterday in Miami. In case you hadn't noticed, it's November in New York." He waited a beat. "And you live a half block from Riverside, the windiest stretch of pavement in the contiguous forty-eight states. What could it hurt to have a look?"

"I hear they got good delicatessens in Miami." This from Sid.

"Wait, there's a problem." Berdie held up her hand. "If Margaret does get the RV, who's gonna drive it?"

"Drive?" Margaret interrupted. "What's the big deal. Oscar used to let me drive the Fraser coming back from the mountains. Every now and then I take my nephew's car for a trip back. I still have my license." She sat up a little straighter in the chair. She looked at the three of them slowly, then for a moment her glance went to the window. "Okay," she finally said, "but just for a look."

CHAPTER 3

...

Damned if the interior wasn't beautiful. Margaret ran her hand along the molded dashboard in front of her, then let it drop to the soft muted fabric of the driver's seat. The smell of newness almost overcame her. It hung in the air in every cubic centimeter of space; the bathroom, the closets, even inside the refrigerator. But what impressed her most, and was so pleasantly unexpected, was the wide expanse of windshield in front of her. Sitting high up, it made her feel almost light-headed as she looked out at the mere people-scaled things in front of her.

"Where's the cream cheese?" Sid asked behind her. "Toasted bagels and no cheese?"

"What am I, the stewardess?" Berdie said. But she got up anyway and made it slowly to the refrigerator. After tugging for a moment, she reached up and threw a little latch. "I keep forgetting. But I suppose if we went around a corner too fast the milk would be in the shower." She brought the container out and made her way back to the dinette table. Sid, sitting next to Durso, already had the knife ready.

"Can you believe the convenience. Every whim right at your fingertips."

"Well, it does take some getting used to," Durso said. "For example, do you know what this button here does?"

Sid shook his head.

"Puts on the roof air conditioner. Says so in the manual. But before you put that one on, you gotta throw the gasoline generator switch. And that one . . ." Durso leaned out of the dinette, his little beret almost tipping off, ". . . is over there by the radio."

Sid squinted toward where Durso was pointing. Berdie was by now back in the front passenger seat watching the streets of New York slowly pass by.

"Like I just said. All the comforts of home. Tea any time, day or night." Sid dipped into the cream cheese and spread it evenly on his bagel. After taking a bite, he turned around and tapped Margaret on the shoulder. "How you doing? It's been almost an hour."

In fact it had been only thirty-eight minutes since Margaret had turned over the 200-horsepower engine and slipped out into traffic. One of the requirements she had insisted on before claiming her prize was that it be delivered to Columbus Avenue. From there it was a straight shot downtown and onto Ninth Avenue and then a simple right turn through the Lincoln Tunnel. She didn't yet trust her left turns across traffic.

In the space of thirty-eight minutes, Berdie had been to the refrigerator five times, Sid to the bathroom to wash his hands twice, and Durso to the microwave oven once. It was only November, but to the four of them, ever since Margaret had agreed a week earlier to accept the Winnebago and head on down to Florida, it was like Christmas morning.

"Piece of cake," Margaret said. "It's no different from the old Fraser." She brought her hand down on the horn as a gypsy cab cut in front of her.

"I still think you should have put in some cornflakes," Berdie said. "I can't make it all the way to Miami on shredded wheat."

"We took a vote," Sid said. "You lost."

"What vote?" Berdie was wide-eyed. "We just chipped in thirty dollars each and sent you to Sloan's."

"Now, now, children," Margaret said from the front. "If Berdie wants cornflakes, at the next grocery stop we'll get her some. We got a long way to go. This thing's only twenty-five feet long, and there are four of us."

Sid looked around the interior of the Winnebago. It sure is amazing what they can do with twenty-five feet, he thought. Along one side of the vehicle was the driver's seat, a deep armchair-looking affair with adjustable arm rests, the dinette with a table for four, the bathroom with a toilet, sink, shower, and a full-length mirror, and at the back an enclosed bedroom with a queen-sized bed. Along the other wall was the passenger seat on a swivel for 360-degree conversations, the door with a second screen door attached, the kitchen area with microwave, double sink, refrigerator, counter top, a huge hanging closet for storage, and the instrument panel for internal operations. On the ceiling was the backup air-conditioning unit and above the driver's/passenger's seats the Pullman berth. Everything else was either window area or covered with cabinets in attractive walnut formica. The floor was overlaid with a deep-pile carpet that was color coordinated with the upholstery of the seats. That's what met the eye, but things were hiding everywhere. A ready-to-use ironing board popped out of one of the cabinets, the dinette converted to a double bed, the kitchen sink cover turned upside down into a chopping block.

"Cornflakes it is," Sid said, looking back to Berdie. "Anything to keep the peace."

Durso was studying the manual. "And that button," he said, pointing, "is the gas heater switch. Hot water we do from outside."

"Good lord," Berdie said. "Who thought it would be so complicated? You have to know a lot."

"You realize what we have here. Nothing short of a

self-contained house," Durso said. "There are systems for waste disposal, temperature control, electrical generation, water supply, food storage and preparation. Two systems each, in fact. One when we pull into a campground at night and hook up to their facilities, and another if we find ourselves marooned in the middle of nowhere. The way I figure it, not including the controls for driving this thing, there are at least eight different kinds of utilities hidden around, each with its own buttons and dials, and unless we know which things do what"—he paused—"tomorrow's coffee might start tasting like yesterday's shower."

"Study away," Sid said. "You're the engineer. I'll be the navigator." He pulled out a bunch of maps and laid them on the table in front of him. He noticed that Margaret was just about to head into the tunnel.

"And me?" Berdie asked.

"Why, I thought that was established," Durso said. "You're the stewardess." Berdie flushed and they all laughed, all except Margaret who was doing her best to bring the Winnebago to an abrupt halt.

"Christ," Sid said as he was thrown backward into the seat. "What's the matter?" He got the question out just as they all heard the scraping noise on the roof.

"I think we have a problem," Margaret said meekly after the Winnebago came to a halt. "Sign on the dashboard says clearance thirteen feet one inch." She sighed. "Sign on that little warning stick at the tunnel entrance says thirteen feet." They all looked at each other. Finally Sid broke the silence.

"Piece of cake, huh. We're not even out of Manhattan."

CHAPTER 4

...

There was a certain amount of unpleasantness at the tunnel. The tow truck operator who hauled them back out and deposited them on the entrance apron left them with two words of advice, "Verrazano Bridge." He also left them with a forty-dollar ticket for not heeding traffic signs. Fortunately the tunnel left only a few scratches on the roof. The thirteen feet one inch must have been for a summer's day with overinflated tires. It was several minutes before Margaret dared speak again.

"Well, who ever looks at those little signs anyway? They're impossible to read." And with that she stepped down harder on the gas and brought the Winnebago up to thirty-five miles an hour.

"Not to worry," Berdie said. "Now we're flying."

■ ■ ■

They made it as far as Chester, Pennsylvania, the first day, only 130 miles but a considerable success since they arrived without incident. By Elizabeth, New Jersey, Margaret had summoned up enough courage to try a left turn. At Carteret she did her first backup out of a diagonal parking space. They lunched just outside New Brunswick and pulled into the campground at Chester a little before three. All four went to assist in the first night's arrangements.

"Full hookup?" the manager asked. "Or partial?" Berdie, Margaret, and Sid turned as one toward Durso.

"Just a moment, just a moment," he begged and went

flipping through the pages of the manual. After a few moments, he had it.

"Full, please, with a pull-through."

The manager nodded casually and studied his map. Obviously they were speaking the same language. He checked off a spot, took their fifteen dollars, and gave them directions.

"No fancy maneuvers I hope," Margaret asked when they were back inside the van.

"No, he gave us the middle row, pull in one side, pull out the other." Durso smiled. "And in case you didn't catch it, full hookup means water, electric, and sewer."

"And partial?"

"No sewer. It's a dollar cheaper."

After a short drive, Margaret pulled into the spot and cut the motor.

"Now," Durso said. "Here's where the fun starts."

In twenty minutes he was finished. Three separate umbilical cords went from the vehicle to sockets around their campsite. Water plug-in near the kitchen, electric just behind the generator, and sewer under the left side toilet. The little gas heater was cooking up hot water for showers and the hot air blower was sending a steady stream of warm air through the inside of the RV. Durso sat down in the dinette as Berdie tentatively turned on the kitchen sink. There was a popping sound, then a steady aerated flow of clear water. Sid and Margaret applauded.

"This," Sid said, "is going to be a great vacation." Without hesitation he reached into one of the cabinets and withdrew a bottle of wine. Berdie provided the four glasses. "A toast," Sid continued. "To the dream-trippers"—he paused,—"and friendship."

They clinked.

"To retirement," Durso added.

They swallowed again.

"Let's not forget Margaret," Berdie said and raised a glass toward her. "Without her, none of this would be possible."

Margaret smiled and touched glasses with the three others.

"And finally," Margaret offered, "to a decent climate."

"Yeah." Sid frowned. "What we got up north is deadly."

CHAPTER 5

...

By the fourth night they were outside Raleigh, North Carolina. Four days of straight sunshine, four nights of complaints. First Sid started in on Margaret's smoking, but when he found her stonewalling, he switched to Berdie's cooking. Durso wondered why he had to sleep in the tiny Pullman, which gave him, he claimed, claustrophobia and vertigo at the same time. Berdie fought back, defending her lasagna with cutting comments about Sid's snoring. And Margaret, not to be singled out on the smoking issue, told Durso if he wanted a pipe now and then, he'd have to hold it out the side window. It became obvious that coexistence was not a skill like bike-riding but one that had to be awkwardly relearned with each new spouse or roommate. In the meantime, no one felt enough at ease to meet any of their nighttime neighbors.

Until Raleigh, where they found themselves drawn up for the night next to a forty-five-foot super-deluxe Southwind with a Cadillac in tow. They were struck at once by the magnitude of the sight and even more surprised when the door opened and Mr. Claiborne "Tiny" Stevens came over to greet them.

"Howdy, folks," he said as he stuck his head in their door. He looked around, apparently was pleased with what he saw, and took a step inside. "Name's Claiborne Stevens. You can call me Tiny." He held out his hand, which, from the look of it, could fell a moose with one blow. "Now who-all do I have the pleasure of inviting over for some barbecue?"

23

*   *   *

"So that's a short rib?" Berdie said looking at the heaping plate of meat in front of them. Six of them were sitting around Mrs. Stevens's dining table, having just finished their cocktails in the forward section of the Southwind. From inside there was little indication they were in a motor home. The living room they had just come from had two modern couches and a pair of chrome and leather easy chairs. Framed pictures of cows hung on the wallpapered walls, and in one open area, a pair of mounted deer hooves held a shotgun and branding rope. Bourbon and branch water had been the offered cocktail.

Mrs. Stevens smiled. "Claiborne can't stand to eat ribs alone. Says it's downright sacrilege." She reached out and passed the platter. "Down in Abilene, leastwise."

"Well, in New York it's pizza," Margaret said. "Makes me awfully lonely ordering just one slice. When Oscar was around, we could finish off a small pie." She reached out and carefully put a few ribs on her plate. She looked at the blackened outside slowly. "How do you get them so . . . authentic?"

"The kitchen has one of those barbecue grills." Mrs. Stevens beamed. "Tiny ordered it special so we can have barbecue even in the rain."

Sid started in on one of them. "Ummm. Maybe we should go to Texas instead of Florida."

"Hell, yes." Tiny said. "You go see Texas, you'll love it. Claire had to pry me away. Damned if it isn't the first vacation for us since we ran our first head of cattle up to Wingate. We're on our way to New York and Montreal. This dang van is as comfortable as all get out and it's easy to drive. I hear parking's pretty difficult in Manhattan so we brought the Caddy just in case." He looked around and frowned. "Hold on here a minute, Claire, where's the bottle of that special wine?"

Mrs. Stevens got up and disappeared into the kitchen area. In a minute she was back with a bottle of Taylor Chablis.

"You sure have good wine in New York. This stuff's hard to come by in Texas. I have it specially flown in."

Durso eyed it skeptically but then held out his glass.

"Hell, all of us old New Yorkers go to Florida," Sid said. "Can't throw in the towel till you've been to Wolfie's."

"You can have your Wolfie's, whatever that is," Tiny said. "I can't wait to see Steeple Chase Park."

Margaret nearly choked. "Good lord, what guidebooks have you been reading?"

Mrs. Stevens poured more wine. "There is one thing I'd like to know," she said eagerly. "Is it true what they say about shopping. I heard the best all-around store is something called John Wanamaker's?"

Margaret looked at her friends. "I think," she said slowly to her two hosts, "we should talk."

■ ■ ■

Three hours and two bottles later, the little party was just breaking up. In that time the four New Yorkers did their best to bring the Stevenses into the eighties. They added some current restaurant recommendations, sightseeing tips, places to shop. They were true New York chauvinists when it came to their city, even when they were escaping from it. Tiny got more than his money's worth, including a recipe for real New York chicken soup from Margaret. In return, the quartet found that drinking with Texans could be amusingly dangerous. Durso, consumed in hiccups and speaking for the rest of them, thanked his hosts, and the four of them tumbled out the door.

"Hey, hold on. Let me show you something," Tiny called out and in a minute was standing by Margaret with his rope. He made a loop at the end and started spinning it over his head. "See that garbage can," he said, and as the New Yorkers turned to look, the rope flew out.

"Bingo. 'Course it wasn't moving and dodging, but it's still pretty good for an old coot of seventy-five." Twenty feet away the loop had gone over the receptacle and now held it securely.

"How'd you do that?" Margaret said.

"It's all in the wrist. Here, let me show you." In a minute he had Margaret spinning the rope over her head with the loop correctly open.

"See, easy, now whynt'cha try to throw it one time."

"I could never . . ." she started, but the Texan held up a hand.

"Try it, it's just a matter of when to release it." He watched her spinning the rope. ". . . Now!"

She opened her hand and the loop went flying out in the direction of the can. It remained open, made one leisurely flip, then landed over the edge of the receptacle. A delighted smile spread across her face.

"I did it! I think the wine helped."

"Sure you did, ain't really too much to it."

Margaret beamed and handed him back his rope. "Good night, Tiny, it was truly a pleasure. I can't remember when I had so much fun."

CHAPTER 6

■■■

In the morning, Tiny had a big hug for the ladies and a crushing handshake for Sid and Durso. Then, like two dinosaurs of a different species, they pulled out of the driveway and went their separate ways. It was their first introduction to that delightful part of touring, the casual intimacy that comes from brief and mostly anonymous encounters.

In Charleston they made friends with a family of four from Detroit, tattooed ex-bikers with two children named Hubcap and Sparky. Hubcap was ten and weighed almost 100 pounds. Unlike his parents, who were cruising America to revisit road scenes from their youth, he was collecting public domain software to plug into his portable computer. In the evening, young Hubcap hacked to his heart's content while munching on an economy-size bag of Doritos. Sparky, Hubcap's eight-year-old brother, was into stamps and had the finest traveling collection of American nineteen-eighties first issue proofs south of Interstate 70. The parents looked on in wonder at the aberrations that were their sons, confessing to Margaret they had no idea where they went wrong. Margaret, drinking a Budweiser out of a Dixie cup, shook her head sadly.

"One never does," she offered.

■■■

The day they made Florida, passing through St. Augustine, Daytona Beach, and finally Fort Pierce, there was a subtle change to the landscape. The colors of the houses changed from the earthy ochres of Georgia and the Carolinas to the pinks, yellows, and turquoises of the Sunshine State. They spotted their first pink plaster flamingo propped up outside a house in Bayard, then, like a plague, one just about every three houses from there. Along with the flamingos, came a proliferation of metal awnings over windows of houses that looked themselves to be made out of nothing more than thin sheet metal. As they drove they were treated to music from radio stations with call letters like W-J-O-Y or W-K-O-S-Y that spewed forth a heavy diet of Percy Faith and Perry Como. Durso referred to them all under one heading—"W-I-M-P-Y." Every now and then a road sign would bring a few guffaws. Sid scored with the "Happy Hocker Pawn Shop," while Durso was the first to spot the one for a kosher steak house. Florida, they all agreed, was something else.

The campsite they pulled into for the night had a swimming pool right out in front. Since it was eighty-three degrees and only four in the afternoon, Durso decided to go in.

"Hell, we're paying for it," he said and rummaged around for his bathing suit. "How about you, Berdie?"

"The last time I had a bathing suit on"—she thought for a moment—"let's see, was July twenty-seventh, 1953."

"You must be kidding. You remember the exact date?"

"Sure, it was the day Tony took me out to Rockaway Beach. Big wave knocked me down and I almost drowned. There I am in the sand gasping for air with Tony doing arm lifts and push-ups on my back and I hear the announcer on the radio talking about the armistice from Panmunjom. Tony kept pumping. Everyone else was shouting and dancing. You don't forget those things. No, you go ahead. I'll just watch."

And he did just that, basking his pallid New York skin in the Florida sun for a good hour and a half. His cotton bathing suit, found after much searching in one of his closets at home, still smelled of mothballs. He had boxes upon boxes of old clothes in the back of his closet with the same acrid smell. He could no longer remember when the first layer on the lowest box had been laid down, but his bathing suit, which came from a stratum somewhere in the middle, reached almost to his knees. And the pattern was something that hadn't been seen since Eisenhower was hooking his tee shots at Burning Tree. Still, he was as happy as a clam when he arrived back at the RV.

"This climate is fabulous. Swimming at five in the afternoon! Back in New York we'd be huddled around our kitchen stoves to keep warm."

"Fish for dinner tonight," Margaret said, changing the subject. "I defrosted the snapper."

"Again fish?" Sid complained. "You're worse than Mary ever was. Least she gave me choices."

"I'll give you a choice." Margaret lit one of her Camels and inhaled deeply. "Frozen snapper with broccoli and rice, or you cook. What'll it be?"

"Given the circumstances," Sid answered, "I'll take mine with lemon and butter."

CHAPTER 7

...

Margaret pulled the big Winnebago onto Collins Avenue and Fourteenth Street, cut the ignition, and slowly rubbed her eyes. It was seven-thirty in the evening, they hadn't eaten dinner yet, and there was no hope for a campsite. They had just spent the last three hours driving to all the KOAs and local campgrounds listed in their guidebooks for Miami. There hadn't been space for even a station wagon, much less a 25-footer.

"Miami Beach at last and not even a partial hookup in miles," Sid groaned. "What the hell, who needs it. We're self-sufficient in here."

"That's right," Margaret concurred. "Might as well stay where we can hear the ocean. No law says we can't park here overnight is there?"

Berdie looked out the front window at the scores of people passing by on the street. "I don't know, Margaret. Seems kind of busy here. Maybe we should go somewhere less active. This is kinda like parking on Broadway."

"Well, I feel safer on Broadway than I do on some empty side street," Durso said.

"Besides, I'm not driving an inch further," Margaret added. "I've gone nearly two hundred miles today, criss-crossed Miami looking for a spot, and now I'm not budging. Joe, put on the generator. Looks like we'll need the air conditioner tonight."

"Hello earth." Sid smiled. "The dream-trippers have landed."

...

The insistent knock came on their door at four-thirty in the morning. After dragging his tired body out of bed, Durso banged his shins on a projecting cabinet edge and opened the door a crack. The policeman who was standing in front of him didn't even bother with a smile.

"I'm sure you'll be happy to move this thing," the man in the crisp uniform said, "and I'm sure it won't take you longer than five minutes. Right?"

Durso, though well versed in the effective use of sarcasm with students, did not understand. Besides, he was bent over rubbing the shin that he was sure had a compound fracture.

"How's that?"

"Get this RV off the street. The hell you think you are parking in the middle of Collins Avenue?"

Durso straightened up. "Officer, there must be some mistake. We're not breaking any law. The meters don't start until eight."

The policeman opened the door, motioned for him to lean out, then pointed up the street.

"Sign says no sleeping in vehicles. City ordinance twenty-five-dash-thirty-three. From the looks of your pajamas, I'd say that pretty much applies to you."

Durso peered at the little blur of white that must have been the sign. Without his glasses, he was lucky to make out the color change. "Geez, I don't think anyone noticed that one." He smiled benignly at the big man with the motorcycle helmet. "You have my sincere apologies."

"Buddy, I don't want your apologies, I want your headlights on and your wheels turning."

"I'm afraid that's impossible," Durso managed. "The driver's asleep. Couldn't this wait until a decent hour . . . say around seven-thirty. Everyone's up and finished breakfast by then."

"Sure we can wait till then, but you'll be breakfasting with a bunch of hookers and pimps that were also picked up during the night. Now, how about it, let's get moving."

A door opened in the back of the RV and Margaret appeared. Her hair was in a net, and she was wearing an old housecoat over her nightgown. She squinted out the door, then went fumbling for her cigarettes.

"What's the matter, we blocking some car?" She couldn't find the pack, and settled for an old butt in one of the ashtrays. After she got it lit, she appeared in the door next to Durso.

"A policeman?" she asked sleepily.

Durso turned back into the van. "He wants us to move. We are apparently in violation of some important city ordinance."

"Don't be a wise guy," the policeman said. "We let motor homes stay on the streets overnight and Miami will look like Yellowstone Park in August. This is a city, not a campground."

"Well, we tried," Margaret offered. She exhaled some smoke and the escaping air-conditioning sucked it outside. "Really we did. There was just nowhere . . ."

"Sorry, you'll have to try again. I can't let you stay here."

"Sure you can," Margaret smiled. "Just keep driving on your rounds. Go find some real criminals like the ones on TV."

"Maybe this will convince you." He pulled his summons book out of his back pocket and with it, a ballpoint pen. "Sorry, lady, you asked for this."

"No, we didn't," Margaret replied with annoyance. "We were sleeping peacefully when you woke us all up. The last time I asked to be woken up in the middle of the night was on my honeymoon forty-five years ago."

Durso let out a bellow. The officer continued writing. "This is ridiculous," Margaret added. "Where do you suppose we could go at five in the morning."

"Not my problem, lady. Maybe you and your husband could take in an all-night drive-in, then check the campgrounds again." His pen kept working.

"For your information," Margaret said hotly, "this gentleman is not my husband. He kindly agreed to come on a trip with me and two others to see the friendly state of Florida. It's obvious we made a terrible mistake." The officer held up the ticket and Margaret grabbed it from him. "Now, tell me the name of your superior. I intend to make a complaint. If this isn't harassment, I don't know what is."

"Look," he said. "One last time. Move it. You're not allowed to stop here. I'll be generous. I'll give you a half hour. If you're not gone by then, I'll take you in." He turned away abruptly and as the two of them watched in silence, he revved up his engine, shifted gears, then took off.

"Think we should go?" Durso asked.

"Certainly not," Margaret said. "He can't wake up peaceful citizens in the middle of the night and get away with it. I want to talk to his boss."

CHAPTER 8

...

Captain Diamond was not the kind of man who lost his temper easily. After thirty years in the Miami police department, he had seen it all from misdemeanors to murder one. Razor blade slashings, adolescent suicides, car accidents that looked like plane wrecks, shoot-outs, street muggings; they were just a few of the things that made up the fabric of his day. He controlled the tenth precinct, which encompassed seventy percent of Miami Beach, with a few odd jerrymandered sections thrown in on the mainland. He had over seventy cops to work with, scores of automobiles, an arsenal that would have made Ma Barker weep, and tactical equipment enough to storm the capital of a small Central American country. With all that, he was facing a mounting drug problem in his precinct that was giving him both insomnia and ulcers and making his local pharmacist a wealthy man.

When Sergeant Moorehead brought in Margaret and her friends it was seven-thirty and Diamond had been at his desk for only twenty minutes. Under the circumstances, he should have done better than to explode only two minutes into the interview.

"Moorehead, you dumb ass, what the hell you bringing these people in here for? What is this, a joke?"

The tall police officer shifted uneasily from one foot to another. "Things just got kinda out of hand," he said. "This lady here refused to leave until she saw you."

"Christ!" Diamond said. "This couldn't be handled by the desk sergeant?" He took a sideways glance at the four

34

senior citizens standing against the back wall. "This is now a church bingo parlor here, right? I don't have enough problems with all the crack that's hitting the street, I gotta play nursemaid too?"

"That's quite enough," Margaret said and stepped forward. In the process she adjusted the little flowery hat she had pinned on top of her head to hide the hair net. "We do not need handholding. An apology will do nicely."

"For what?" Diamond, under the best circumstances, never liked giving apologies.

"For employing and encouraging the kind of officers who harass senior citizens. This gentleman here should be demoted to patrolling a kiddie park."

Diamond looked at Moorehead with a scowl, then back to Margaret.

"Look," he said trying to control his voice. "The law says you can't stay there. He was only trying to do the job the people of this city pay him to do. You don't like the law, go to Palm Beach. I'd be surprised if they even let you drive your RV through town." Sid was about to say something when Diamond held up his hand. "Now you'll understand that I can't spend all day on this. I got people dying in this town, which, believe me, takes priority over your particular parking problem." He turned to Moorehead. "Next time, see if you can't deal with this outside."

"Oh, so now you think you've dealt with this?" Margaret said, fuming. "You just kicked four helpless seniors out of town, because I can guarantee there won't be space at any RV park today just like there wasn't any yesterday. Do you think the papers will like that? 'Miami, retirement community to the nation, begins ejecting senior citizens.'"

Diamond sighed and leaned back in his chair. Margaret couldn't help thinking how much like Lee Iococca he looked. Except Lee Iococca didn't pack a .38 Special at his waist and wear clothes that said somewhere on them, "machine wash, tumble dry."

"Listen lady, I'll tell you a story. Twenty years ago I'm flying on a plane to Chicago. There's this bag in the aisle blocking the stewardesses. So they start coming around asking whose it is. First one passenger, then another, and they all say the same thing . . . 'Sorry, it's not my suitcase.' They come to me and I say the same thing. I've been using that ever since." He rocked forward and stood up. "Sorry, lady, it's not my suitcase. Moorehead, show them to the exit. See if you can work something out." He hesitated for a moment. "Be creative." He came around the side of the desk and without saying another thing walked through a side door and left them. Moorehead motioned and then ushered them out into the hall.

"I told you," he said. "Diamond is not a guy with much patience. We could have worked something out without your going in there."

"So, work something out," Sid said. "But we didn't drive all the way from New York to wind up in some RV park in the Everglades."

"Isn't there someplace we can stay for just a few nights?" Berdie asked politely. "It's really Miami we came to see."

Moorehead rubbed the bridge of his nose with two fingers, then looked back at them. "Not on Collins Avenue there isn't. The merchants and innkeepers would be down on us like flies. You picked just about the worst place to stop."

"So, show us a better one." Durso said.

The sergeant looked at them closely, then shook his head. "My luck I pulled the lobster shift this week. Okay, follow me. We're going south on Collins, then west a little bit on Second. There's a strip there I think you could stop at. It's pretty safe . . . near the beach . . . out of my hair." He grinned at Margaret. "Then I could go out and chase some real hardened types."

"Thank you, Officer Moorehead," Margaret said, grinning back. "I'll take that as a form of apology."

CHAPTER 9

...

Moorhead led them south along Collins Avenue past what was once the glory of Miami Beach. Starting around Nineteenth Street they drove by dozens of Art Deco architectural gems, hotels with names like the Fairmont, and the Essex House. At one time their tropical pastel hues had lured the wealthy to bask in their gracious, modern interiors. Now, the best they could do was catch sloppy seconds off the retirement trade. The pastel limes and raspberries and pinks were still in place, punctuated by round windows and bold stripes of molding, but behind the facades the grandeur had long since faded. For Sale signs littered the tiny lawns of many of the smaller establishments. Even the larger hotels showed signs of wear: neon signs with an odd letter not working, rusting patio chairs, grey asphalt driveways cracked with weeds. The whole South Beach area was one visual irony; bypassed by the economics of scale and glitz, it remained an anachronism of abiding charm.

Moorehead stopped at a spot west of Collins on Second, told them they had his blessings, then took off with the muffled roar that only a 1000-cc Harley could produce. The Winnebago, left alone on the street of small-scale two- and three-story buildings, looked somewhat outsized. There were wide gaps between the few cars parked against the curb.

"Can you believe this?" Margaret said looking out of the front window. "They're all 'efficiencies' or 'Pull-manettes.'"

Her three friends came up front and looked out. The

little establishments marched along both sides of the street in perfect order. In the front of each one ran a porch with no less than ten aluminum lawn chairs. Like a string of pearls, this line of chairs, with their occupants, encircled the street. While they watched, the human necklace undulated ever so slightly as the old-timers leaned back and forth. Every head was turned their way, every eye peering at the large intruder on the block. Margaret went to the little bedroom in back and looked out the rear window. What she saw made her gasp. Another street, then another, with the same endless array of lawn chairs and old people.

"My God," she said. "How long do you think they'll sit there?" She looked at her watch. "It's only nine o'clock."

"Probably all day," Sid said. "But don't they look all done in."

"If that's retirement, Florida style, I'll take New York any day," Berdie offered.

Very few of the people on the porches moved from their chairs, and then only to change to another one positioned more in the sun. On the street two old men walked slowly together.

"This can't be typical." Durso said. "I always thought Florida meant condos and swimming pools."

Sid chuckled. "Looks like a lot of people didn't get the prospectus." He pulled back from the window. "I don't know about you, but I think I want to see a little more of this city than a bunch of old geezers stirring the air. How about we walk a little bit on Collins Avenue, then go down to the beach?"

They all agreed, but Margaret had a hard time pulling herself away from the window.

"You never see this on TV," she said as she rubbed a little face powder on. "Just white jackets and fast boats."

*   *   *

They made it all the way up to Wolfie's for lunch and then
after some more window-shopping, found a wonderful little
public park to rest in during the hot part of the afternoon.
Collins Avenue above Twenty-third Street was a lot different from what it was near the Winnebago. Farther north
the condos Durso had mentioned were in such great numbers they walled off the ocean.

To Margaret, Miami Beach appeared to be two cities,
or maybe one city and one ghetto. She had a hard time
losing the image of all those lawn chairs and their forlorn
occupants. When they finally stepped off the bus back on
Second Street, the scene, if anything, had become even
more oppressive. Walking to the Winnebago was like walking through a gauntlet of depression.

"They never move," Margaret said.

"They gotta eat," Berdie pointed out. "And sleep."

"And nothing else." Margaret shook her head. "It's a
living graveyard." She stopped when she reached the van
and looked to her right. They were parked by the Glenmore Rest House which, like all the others, had several of
its tenants on the porch. Margaret studied the dozen or so
faces of the men and women, all of whom were looking
expressionlessly at her. Her eyes lingered on one, a woman
who had a fringe of copper-colored wiry hair and a face
that looked as though it had been through too many cold
winters. As Margaret stared, the woman's face opened up
and the tiniest of smiles crossed her lined features. She held
it just long enough for Margaret to see it, then it was gone.
Margaret nodded softly back, turned, and entered the van.

"I get the feeling," she said after a moment of removing
her shoes, "that they're all trapped. It's like some bizarre
Stephen King setting."

"To be old in America"—Durso shook his head—"was never a blessing."

Margaret opened the refrigerator and brought out the defrosted chicken wings. But the entire time she went through the motions of preparing them for the frying pan, she had a removed, thoughtful expression on her face. Finally, when they were sizzling in the half inch of oil and the package of frozen peas in butter sauce was boiling in a saucepan, she sat down at the little dinette and looked over at Sid.

"What were we planning to do tomorrow?" she asked innocently.

"I dunno, I thought perhaps a trip to one of the malls. They're supposed to be like little cities."

"Mmmmmm," Margaret said slowly. "I think there will be a slight change of plans."

CHAPTER 10

...

It took almost an hour over dinner, plus a few glasses of sherry, but Margaret finally convinced the three of them to go along with the scheme. Early next morning, they found themselves on the porch of the Glenmore Rest House facing the handful of tenants. Margaret had already obtained the manager's approval for what she was about to propose.

"We are offering free sightseeing rides," she began, "in our Winnebago." There was a little murmur from the group in front of her. "We can take about eight people, but I guarantee it will be the most comfortable sightseeing ride you've ever been on. There are couches and tables to sit at, a toilet for your convenience, and a kitchen with coffee and Danish throughout the morning. There's even a bed in case you want to take a nap. And," she added, "you tell us where you want to go. We'll drop you back here at noon." She looked around but no one moved. "And plenty of conversation . . . we even listen to stories of grandchildren. How about it?" She came over and stood in front of the woman with the copper-colored hair. She lowered her voice. "It's all free."

The other woman peered into Margaret's eyes, apparently saw something there that reassured her, and nodded her head slowly.

"Ja," she answered. "I go. I alvays vanted to see Hollavood." She gave Sid her hand, and with a little help, stood up and walked to the steps. Within two minutes, her six porch neighbors were walking down the stairs behind her and heading for the open door of the Winnebago.

"I hope they enjoy it," Berdie said to Durso as they trailed behind.

"Listen, just getting them off that porch was a success."

■ ■ ■

They did two tours that day, and two the next day, and when they were finished, everyone at the Glenmore Rest House had been aboard. The RV crisscrossed Miami, went north to Hollywood, west to Hialeah, south to Coral Gables, and stopped at several of the delicatessens in between. Inside the van there was an atmosphere of excitement as the passengers pointed out various places they were familiar with or had always wanted to see. Everyone was delighted with the accommodations, even with the toilet, and told Margaret that it was the best thing that had happened to them in years. The four New Yorkers were just as enthusiastic; every trip was different, with different sights and different people to chat with. The only problem was that news of the excursions had spread to several of the other guest houses. Early on the morning of the third day, a small group of guest-house owners came to speak with them. The owners asked, with great politeness, whether they might see their way to expanding the excursions to include some of the other establishments.

"You can't imagine how much all of our guests are looking forward to it," the owner of the Sea Breeze Rest Home said. "It's the best thing that's happened in years."

Margaret looked at her friends and shrugged. "How about it?"

"I'm game for another week at least," Durso said.

"Me too," Berdie concurred.

"I guess we'll need a name," Sid said with a grin. "Something catchy."

There was silence for a moment as the few guest-house owners looked blankly at each other.

"I know," Durso said. "How about the Dream-trippers Coach and Excursion Society."

"Perfect," Margaret said. "Now all we need is a sign and we're in business."

CHAPTER 11

...

Within a week the *Miami Herald* had covered it. There had been so much talk from one rest house to another that it was inevitable someone would leak it. The story ran in the features section alongside a photograph of the four New Yorkers mugging it up outside the door of the Winnebago. The caption read "Manhattanites bring sunshine to Second Street" and the article went on to describe their humanitarian efforts with the van. While Sid and Berdie basked in their transient fame, the article got the dream-trippers more attention than they needed. They already had a waiting list of rest homes expecting their visit. The day after the article appeared, they got messages from five more with requests. Margaret figured they could make a career out of it. While no money changed hands, all the establishments were more than happy to provide box lunches, send cleaning people to straighten up the Winnebago after an excursion, and, what was most important, donate free gas. It was amazing how cooperative everyone was.

But Margaret kept things strictly informal. Every morning they set out from the same spot on Second Street and pulled up unannounced in front of one of the guest houses on their list. Some of them were small and they could take everyone at one time, sometimes it took two or even three excursions. At the end of the day, their guests left them with little mementos: chocolates they had been saving, favored scarves or delicately embroidered handkerchiefs, little drawings—anything that helped them say thank you. As far as Margaret was concerned, they were quite unnecessary. She was having too much fun to need any of it. The Dream-trippers Coach and Excursion Society was a natural, loved by proprietor and customer alike and fulfilling a need so obvious it was shocking it had not been met before.

On Wednesday of the second week they were returning from an excursion when Margaret made an unexpected turn along North Bay Road. It was a street of expensive residences mixed among some twenties Art Deco hotels that backed onto Biscayne Bay. As they headed south, one of the guests they were shepherding around pointed out the window and said wryly, "I don't expect you'll be getting much of a reception there." Berdie looked to where he was pointing and noticed a large, beautifully restored guest house painted gray and pink. A sign over the front door discreetly announced that they were looking at Forstman's Rest Home.

"Nice setting," Berdie said. "Right on the water."

"'S what I thought," the elderly man continued. "But when I looked into becoming one of their tenants, it was like I was applying for a job with the CIA. What didn't they ask, especially about how was I gonna pay." He laughed to himself. "I told this guy, this Forstman fella, I told him it was Social Security all the way. No bank accounts, no rich relatives, no pensions, nothing but three ninety-two fifty a month. I was out the door faster than you can say bum's rush."

"That's surprising," Margaret said from the front seat. "Most of the owners we've met are so polite." The Winnebago coasted to a stop at a red light and Margaret looked at a little notebook she had beside her. "Let's see, what's the name?"

"Forstman's," Berdie said.

Margaret traced a finger down the column of names. "Nope, you're right. They haven't asked."

"If they haven't," Sid said, "they're one of the few that haven't. Looks like there are over twenty names there."

"Twenty-three," Durso corrected. "Let's be accurate."

"Oh well," Margaret said absently. "They probably have enough activities to keep their people involved. Did you notice anyone on the porch?"

"No chairs," the man who had pointed out the hotel said. "A nice wide porch with no chairs. I remember noticing it at the time."

"That's peculiar," Margaret said softly, and turned left onto Second Street. In another minute she pulled to a stop and turned off the motor.

"Here we are," Sid said. "Windemere Apartments, last stop."

After hugs and handshakes, the Floridians filed off the bus. Margaret got out of the driver's seat, switched on the auxiliary generator and then the air-conditioning, and sat back down slowly.

No porch chairs, she thought with a frown.

CHAPTER 12

...

The Winnebago pulled up in front of Forstman's Rest Home at nine o'clock the next morning. After seventy-two years of living in a city that required extrasensory perception for street survival, Margaret's sensors were acting up. Not ringing really, just twitching, the same way they did when the doctor had asked Oscar to come back for further routine blood tests. Poor Oscar, she thought. Parkinson's at sixty-five, just as he reached the best years of his life.

She couldn't remember how often she had felt the same way. On any of the cases with Lieutenant Morley of the Eighty-second Precinct of course. The time Thelma got in trouble with her landlord and that awkwardness with the garden. So, while an old-age guest home without porch chairs was not particularly unlawful, it was surprising enough to arouse Margaret's curiosity. Besides, she wondered what it was that set Forstman's apart from the other dozens of guest homes anxious for the Dream-trippers.

"Durso and I will go in," she said opening the side door. "We don't need to overpower them. The sign, Sid. Don't forget to put it in the side window facing them. Let them know who we are." With that she stepped out and, with Durso trailing, marched up to the front door. For the moment, that's as far as she got.

The door they were facing was made of heavy metal with a glass panel in the top. It was not unlike many of the other doors on similarly styled guest houses in the area, except that it was locked. Margaret pushed, then Durso pushed, then they pushed together. As they were slowly digesting the fact that it was unaccountably locked, a tiny loudspeaker interrupted them.

"What do you want?"

Margaret took a step back, rose up to her full five feet two inches and replied without a pause, "Entrance." Then she straightened her cotton dress nervously and pushed the hat on her head a little straighter as she waited for a reply.

"What for?"

Margaret peered through the glass panel but couldn't see anyone. Then Durso pointed to a little television camera high up.

"Excuse me," she said, turning just a little toward the speaker. "If you find me threatening I cannot imagine what you are doing in this business. I'm seventy-two, quite harmless, and, I assure you, not carrying a concealed weapon." She faced forward again and waited. In a short time a buzzer sounded somewhere near the lock, and the door swung in a few inches.

"Come in," the speaker said after them. "First door on the left."

The door closed behind them by itself and the noise it made reminded Margaret of the ending of that old television show, "Dragnet"; the large law book closing with a thud on another unlucky criminal. But they were inside and they found the first door on the left without any problem. Perhaps it was because of the little metal sign over the door that said Office. More probably it was because of the man standing by the doorframe studying them as they came forward. To Margaret he looked like the Greek counterman at Stark's coffee shop in New York, thin face, petulant mouth. His posture was casual, but his eyes said, "I'm waiting, make it good." His voice took the middle ground.

"What is it?" he asked. "We're not a transient hotel."

"No, and we're not looking for a room," Margaret said politely. "We'd like to speak to the manager."

"And we don't donate to any local causes; pet hospitals, little league, school newspapers, things like that. If you're after a solicitation, I'm afraid I can't help you." The man tried to smile but they could see it was clearly an effort. He was in his forties, well tanned, and with enough gold around his neck to open up a jewelry counter at the local JC Penney's.

"Such an open mind," Durso piped up from behind Margaret.

"How's that?"

"Nothing," Margaret said and shot a disapproving glance behind her. "Mr. Durso and I are with the Dream-trippers Coach and Excursion Society and have decided to come to your hotel this morning." As if there could be any doubt as to just who the Dream-trippers were, Margaret unfolded the newspaper clipping from her handbag and gave it to the other man. "I know you haven't requested we come, but here we are anyway." She closed her handbag softly, and while the man with the jewelry read the article, took the luxury of looking around.

The downstairs of Forstman's rest house was spare. A green carpet runner lead from the front door along a central corridor off which were three other rooms and a few closed doors. There were several chairs along the wall, all of which were empty. The office was opposite a large living room decorated in what could only be described as Florida Danish. There were a lot of dark tapered wooden legs and flowered upholstered seats, some wicker, and a great deal of vinyl. The pictures on the walls were all of sailboats, that eternal metaphor for freedom. It looked as if the owner had bought a dozen at a quantity discount. They also alluded to the proximity of the water, which was, as Margaret noticed, right outside the living room window.

But if a free-floating, windswept spirit was the aesthetic of the Forstman establishment, its tenants certainly hadn't gotten the message. Margaret was appalled at the look on the faces of all the people huddled in the living room, most of whom by now were carefully observing the three of them. A more abject group of senior citizens she had yet to see. There was a sense of depression in that room so thick you could plaster the walls with it. No one said anything— they just stared—but to Margaret their silence was eloquent enough. If old people did anything, they talked; they kibitzed, they kidded, they gossiped, they bragged, they did most of their living in dialogue. But at Forstman's, you could hear a pin drop.

"Sorry, we're not interested," the man with the chains said. "But thanks anyway."

"But," Margaret said with some confusion, "it's all free. Take a look, the Winnebago is right outside."

"No, thank you," the man repeated. "Our guests are quite content to remain with us." He handed her back the newspaper clipping. "They have all the conveniences they need right at hand. We keep them so happy, there's not a single vacancy." He nodded to the front door. "Perhaps the Sheridan Guest House down the block has people who are unhappy with their daily activities, but we don't. Good day."

"That's a pity," Margaret said. "We've had a lot of happy people ride with us, but then I guess you know your guests better than we do." She turned toward the front door and Durso followed her. After taking a few steps, she turned back and stopped the man as he was going back into the office. "One little favor," she asked with the tiniest note of urgency. "Would it be possible for me to use your bathroom? We haven't had a chance yet to fill up the water tank. It had such heavy use yesterday."

The younger man thought about it for a few seconds, then shrugged and nodded down the hallway. "Make it fast," he said and popped back into the office.

"I'll only be a minute," she told Durso loudly and disappeared into the bathroom. Durso took a seat and waited. Very shortly the sound of someone dialing the telephone could be heard coming from the office, followed by the man's voice. It didn't take much eavesdropping to figure out the nature of the call. Mr. Fourteen-karat was trying to set up a date for the night and was running into some resistance. Out of the corner of his eye, Durso saw Margaret open the bathroom door and slowly sneak down the hallway. There was no other word for it. She stayed against the wall next to the office and after hesitating for only a second, slipped around the door frame into the living room. The conversation on the phone continued without interruption but Durso felt his heart thump. Good Lord, he wondered, now what's she up to? From where he was he couldn't see into the living room and so decided to stay where he was. He looked at his watch nervously. Nine-fifteen.

At nine-twenty he heard the phone being hung up and a moment later, the man appeared at the doorway. It must have slipped his mind that the two of them were still there because when he saw Durso, he frowned and said quickly, "She still inside?"

"No, Mr. Forstman, I'm in here," they both heard her say. "Talking with some of your contented guests."

"What the . . ." Forstman started, and took the four steps over into the doorway of the living room. Durso followed. "Who said you could talk to anyone?"

Margaret was sitting on a couch and had four or five people around her. When Forstman came in they seemed to shrink back ever so slightly in their seats. Margaret waved his question away and in the same gesture, indicated the others in the room.

"There seems to be a great deal of interest in sightseeing trips. I merely mentioned the possibility and several of your guests reacted favorably. I think you should perhaps reconsider our offer."

"No, I think you should get out," Forstman responded. "You are now trespassing."

"But your guests . . ." Margaret continued.

"Take advice from me. And I say they are not going." He took two further steps into the room and glowered at all of them. "Unless there is anyone here who still wants to go on this implausible sightseeing trip. How about it." He looked at each one in turn. "Any takers?"

The room was silent except for a little fan on a side table. No one moved. Finally, a man with white hair and eyes that looked like pools of melted ice stood up and limped forward. His face was lined and haggard, but the eyes didn't waver.

"I don't understand, Mr. Forstman. They're just trying to do something nice for us."

"I said no, Mr. Schecter." He looked at the other man threateningly. After a moment, the older man nodded, then walked sadly out of the room. Forstman looked back at Margaret. "There's your answer. Now, please . . . get out."

"I think not," Margaret said. "I'm not finished talking to these people."

"Oh no?" Forstman said. He turned, walked into the office, and pushed a little black button on his desk. Almost immediately, another door in the corridor opened and an attendant appeared. At the sight of him Durso caught his breath. He had always thought of white-coated people as helpful, somewhat antiseptic, and, at the very worst, innocuous. Waiters, oral hygienists, lab technicians, beauticians at Macy's; they all fell into the same neutral to positive category. But there was nothing innocuous about the giant Forstman had brought out of the closet. Six foot two if he was an inch, and with a face that made Charles Bronson look like a high school prom queen. This was no yuppie intern at Miami General, unless he was specializing in facial reconstruction. He took a step closer and asked Forstman for directions.

"Those two," Forstman pointed. "I want them out."

"We were just going," Durso said quickly. "Isn't that right Margaret?" He grabbed her hand and started to lead her out of the room. She held back a little, but Durso wouldn't have it. He pulled her into the corridor with the white-coated attendant following. When they were still five feet away from the front door, the buzzer sounded and it slowly opened inward. As they were about to pass through, the white-haired older gentleman with the cold blue eyes got up from a chair nearby and came quickly over to Margaret. He shook her hand and said, loud enough for everyone to hear, "Do come again. Perhaps we will have changed our minds by then."

"Just a minute," Forstman yelled from down the corridor.

But it was too late. By the time it registered with the attendant following them, both Durso and Margaret were outside and making their way off the porch. The big man came outside after them, but stopped when he saw the traffic on the street in front of the rest house. It wouldn't do to have one of Forstman's staff seen bashing heads on their lawn. He watched as the two made it to the curb and quickly entered the van. Then he turned back into the house as his boss caught up with the older man. Even from a distance of over forty yards, Margaret and Durso and the two others in the Winnebago heard Forstman's repeated question, right up until the front door slammed and choked off his raised voice, "What was it, Schecter, damn it? What did you give her?"

Durso looked at Margaret and raised an eyebrow. She shrugged and slowly opened her hand. In it was a piece of paper folded several times.

"You read about these things," Durso said softly. "In mystery books."

CHAPTER 13

...

"Prisoners . . . since The Eternal Holidaze"

The four of them looked at the little piece of paper on the dinette table and puzzled over its message.

"Not very good at spelling, is he?" Berdie offered. "Holidaze indeed."

"Maybe it's a code," Durso suggested. "In case Forstman got it from us."

Margaret sat back. "It's obvious all is not well in that establishment. Even without this note, that place gave me the creeps. Did you see how they all reacted to him . . . like he had some kind of power over them." She tapped the paper in front of her. "Prisoners is right."

"You don't really think they can't come and go as they please?" Sid asked. "I mean it's only a rest home, not a jail."

"You should'a seen the fancy locks on the doors," Durso said. "And the way that guy squashed any of them from going out with us."

"The question is," Sid offered, looking at the three others, "what the hell should we do about it?"

"That's easy," Margaret said. "Go to the police. What's his name, Captain Diamond. I'm sure he'll be interested."

"What makes you so sure?" Sid asked.

"Because that's his job," Margaret answered. "To protect the citizens of his city."

Durso chuckled. "Good lord, Margaret, haven't you learned anything in seventy-two years? You think Miami is any different from New York?"

She glared at him for a moment. "Well, we'll just have to see, won't we." She stood up and moved to the driver's seat. "Come on, buckle up."

■ ■ ■

The South Miami Beach police headquarters was located in a building of postwar design on Fifth and Meridian. "Design" was a generous description, since the building was a windowless pile of concrete badly in need of a whitewashing. The only color around was a United States flag that hung listlessly over a sign that said Tent Pre inct. Two struggling palm trees framed the entrance as obliging reminders that this was a sunny Florida police station and not some air raid shelter in Minnesota. Right next door was the Miami Beach Body Shop, which looked in much better condition. At least its sign had all its letters.

They had been inside the building once before, but this time Margaret looked around more carefully. Even though miles apart, there were many similarities with the Eighty-first in New York; the gum-chewing patrolmen who clustered languidly outside doorways waiting for the slow process of justice to proceed, the slack-eyed collars handcuffed and bored, the dozens of half-empty coffee cups resting on chairs, tables, and the floor. In the background the clatter of typewriters lent a little rhythm to the proceedings. Decorous it wasn't, but the South Miami Beach headquarters was open for business.

Margaret found Diamond's office without any problem; but getting past his young deskman was another matter. By sheer luck, during their little discussion, Diamond himself emerged on his way to the coffee machine. Margaret gave up with the fresh-faced kid and turned on him right away. Without giving him a chance, she hit him with her standard opener.

"I did it, just like you said, but it didn't work."

Diamond stopped, looked her up and down, then bent a little closer. He hesitated for only a second. "Did what?"

"Brought it here to show you, but your guard dog here didn't want you to see it."

Diamond straightened, glanced over at the desk, then turned back. "Why is that?"

"Search me," Margaret said. "Everyone thinks it's important."

"What the hell is she talking about," he finally blurted out to the young officer at the desk. "Am I supposed to know something here?"

The clerk shook his head and started to get up.

"No appointment and some crazy story . . ."

"Can we talk?" Margaret interrupted. "In the time this is taking I could have it out already."

Diamond turned back and looked at the little group.

"Something is registering," he said. "Haven't I seen you before?"

"Inside would be better," Margaret continued. "Away from all this noise. Five minutes is all I ask. You were probably on your way to get coffee anyway."

"I was, and still am," Diamond said and took the few steps over to the machine. He pulled out a cup and dumped in some liquid. "Okay," he said finally over his shoulder. "But only five minutes."

"In that case," she said. "I'll take some too. Light . . . no sugar."

■ ■ ■

It actually took them seven minutes to tell their story. Durso kept interrupting and amplifying on little details and

Margaret kept pushing the note under Diamond's nose, but in the end, of course, he wasn't the least bit interested.

"No law was broken," he said simply. "No reason for the police to interfere."

"But it says they're prisoners," Margaret replied incredulously. "You can't just drop it."

"Who can't. Listen, lady, there are more certifiable loonies in South Miami Beach than there are gamblers in Vegas. One thinks he's Napoleon, one thinks she's Marie Antoinette. Maybe if they're lucky they'll find each other. Your luck, you found one that thought he was Sir Walter Raleigh."

"Very funny," Margaret said. "I'm not laughing."

"Besides," he said. "I just remembered. You're the bunch Moorehead brought in . . . what was it, for camping out on Collins with a Winnebago."

"Right," Berdie said with a smile and searched in her handbag for a copy of the article. They each had their own copy.

"That's nice," Diamond said, "very nice." He put down his empty coffee cup. "But here's another clipping, one I gotta deal with every day." He reached in his desk and brought out a piece of acetate with a scrap of newsprint inside. The headline said, "Crack Use up Forty Percent, Justice System Overburdened." Diamond continued. "You want to talk about clippings." He leaned back in his chair. "I got plenty more clippings if you want to see them, but I think you get the idea. I don't have too much time to go checking up on the sanity of rest home tenants. You want to do something, take it to the agency that licenses them . . . the State Health and Rehab Services. They got inspectors. Convince one of them the place is an old-age Alcatraz and let them handle it. I'm sorry, but I can't. And now, coffee break's over, time to get back to work."

"I don't believe it," Margaret said, flushing.

"I do," Durso said. "Come on, let's go. "Police are the same all over."

"Close the door on the way out," Diamond called after them. "And enjoy the rest of your stay in Miami."

CHAPTER 14

...

On the way out they met Moorehead. The younger officer, unlike his boss, took no time in recognizing them.

"What the hell you doing here?" he asked. "Don't tell me you moved back north onto Collins."

"I can't go into it again," Margaret said tiredly. "You tell him, Joe."

Moorehead listened to Durso. At the end he shook his head.

"Eternal Holidaze . . ." Moorehead squinted. "Sounds like it could be the name of a boat."

"A boat . . ." Margaret said softly. "And they're right on the water. Yes, I think that's it. Thank you, Moorehead, thanks a lot."

"Not that that will do you any good," Moorehead continued. "There've got to be over ten thousand boats in the Miami area alone. It would be hard to find the whereabouts of any particular one."

"It would," Margaret said. "Unless you had a lot of free time." She turned to her three friends. "Perhaps, for the moment, the Dream-trippers should suspend operations. Temporarily, of course."

"Are you planning what I think?" Berdie asked.

"Margaret's eyes twinkled. "Who else is going to do it?"

...

They started methodically, going into every marina along the eastern side of Biscayne Bay starting from the Mac-

61

Arthur Causeway. The story they had concocted about losing the address of the marina but remembering the name of the boat worked well. No one liked to keep a grandma or grandpa from a child's birthday party, which was the backbone of their story. They took turns playing the grandparent until 1:00 P.M. when, from sheer exhaustion, they had to stop for lunch. By that time they had canvassed ten marinas and not one had ever heard of a boat called *The Eternal Holidaze*. Dispirited, the four New Yorkers parked on one of the roads parallel to the water and sat down to chicken salad sandwiches and coffee. Berdie kicked off her shoes and let her feet sink into the soft pile of the Winnebago's carpet.

"This is like looking for a needle in a haystack," she said between bites. "Only difference is we're not even sure it's a needle we're after. How long do you figure we should give it?"

"As long as it takes," Margaret said. "If it is a boat, someone will have heard of it. It's got to be pretty big." She massaged the back of her neck and looked out the window. "Trouble is, all these little inlets and private docks. It could be just about anywhere."

As she watched, a large Bertram yacht glided past with a powerful, throaty sound to its engines. Her eyes followed it until she could read the name on the stern. "Good lord," she said. "You'd think every high school yearbook caption writer had found careers in the boat-naming business. That one was called *She Lost Again*. That's almost as cute as the one we saw at the last marina, that sailboat called *Deep Float*. I ask you, why do they always have to be so awfully cute?"

"What did you have in mind?" Sid asked.

"Well, you know, something with a little more dignity,

something like"—she thought for a moment—"*The Queen Mary.*"

"Classy," Durso said and started filling his pipe. "How about *Titanic II*? That should get a few guffaws from the overpasses."

"I was not being facetious," Margaret said pointedly. "Those names are really silly, and mostly disrespectful to women on top of everything."

"It's true," Berdie added. "You never see a boat named *The Helpless Husband,* or *The Birdbrained Bachelor,* do you. How come?"

"Because it's men who buy the boats," Sid said. "And I never met a man who didn't get just the tiniest little bit of pleasure needling the opposite sex."

"Once a chauvinist, always a chauvinist," Margaret grumbled. "If you were forty years younger you couldn't get away with that stuff."

"If I were forty years younger"—Sid grinned"—I'd be getting away with better stuff."

CHAPTER 15

...

There was nothing new about being yelled at by Forstman. Schecter recalled at least a dozen times in the last month when Forstman had exploded at someone for the most minor infraction of the hotel rules. Not that there were all that many; the three main ones being no outgoing telephone calls without permission, no visits from relatives unless cleared first, and no walks without an attendant. But Forstman even got annoyed over things like loud radios, fraternizing with the delivery boys, or heated conversations among the guests in the lounge. All of these rules were ostensibly to protect the serenity of the institution and the health of its patients. In fact what they did was to imprison everyone. Not that it mattered to most of his fellow inmates, Schecter had to admit, most of whom had no family or outside friends. Which was peculiar in itself given the fact that older people tend to leave a trail of friendships and relatives behind them. To Schecter, most of the others at Forstman's seemed to be walking around in a fog. Maybe that's how you got after a few years in the place. Or maybe that's how you got after repeated attempts to leave the premises were met with strong reproofs and delaying excuses. Now, after six months of it, Schecter decided he had had enough. It was not so bad when he had arrived, but it got worse after that boat made an appearance. For six hundred dollars a month he didn't have to be treated like an incarcerated criminal. That's why he had to say something to that nice-looking older woman, even if it meant getting yelled at by Mr. Forstman.

But the strange part was that the yelling stopped almost before it began. Forstman asked what he had handed the woman, and when he realized he wasn't going to get an answer, he had quietly turned away. Very uncharacteristic.

Schecter looked at his watch and saw it was getting close to noon. That meant lunchtime. Probably chipped beef again. It also meant his goddamn battery of pills. He got up slowly from the easy chair in the hallway and headed to his own room. There they were, as always, the little shining reds and yellows and multicolor nasties sitting in their ubiquitous paper cups. Forstman's staff attendants doled them out on schedule, treating all the patients like untrustworthy adolescents. The only way he could get them down any more was with the vodka he had cleverly hidden in his top drawer. Schecter turned over one of the tiny containers into his palm and threw the two pills into his mouth. He took a swig of Smirnoff from the glass he had waiting, then popped two more pills from another paper cup. T. S. Eliot had it wrong. Life was not measured in spoonfuls, but in capsules. He turned back into the corridor and headed toward the dining room. The smells coming from the kitchen told him he had been right—chipped beef it was.

Of course nothing would come of his note to that lady. What could she do? Still, it made him feel good. Hell, just to get Forstman's anger up. Maybe when that boat went away . . . the one that Franco went to visit every now and then in that pedal boat. Oh yes, they tried to be clever about it, but he had seen, he knew.

He sat down at the table and in a few minutes was joined by Mrs. Epping and Jonas Fletcher. Without taking much notice of each other, they started their noonday meal.

CHAPTER 16

...

After three more marinas, they ran into a stretch of private docks along the waterway where they could drive slowly and see the names of all the boats. But at least one out of every four slips was empty, and so they had to stop whenever they saw an owner on board and ask if they could fill in some information.

So it was that after two hours and more than thirty blocks of surveyed waterfront, they came abreast of *The Mighty Moe,* a twin-engine 400-horsepower Roballo that was almost ten feet longer than their van. It rested low in the water and looked as if it could outrun most anything that floated. For all that length, most of the boat was open. It was obviously not built along the lines of a family weekender, fat-waisted and wallowy, but rather for the likes of a well-tanned Italian industrialist on the Eleuthera/Costa Esmeralda circuit. Margaret noticed some activity at the stern, and for the tenth time since lunch, got out to ask her questions. The surprise in her face was evident when a pair of the friendliest white-haired heads appeared over the transom. In less time than it takes to say "hop on board," Margaret was shaking hands with Mr. and Mrs Carl Manuzzi from Paterson, New Jersey. The Manuzzis were, from the sound of it, on their way out. The motors were running and all the canvas had been laid back.

"I'll be brief," Margaret began, and asked about the nearby empty slips. Mrs. Manuzzi, seeing the fatigue on her face, sat her down, offered her a cold drink, and had the entire story out in five minutes.

"Can't say I've heard of her," Mr. Manuzzi confessed. "*The Eternal Holidaze* you said?" He scratched his chin, which looked as if it hadn't seen a razor in over forty-eight hours.

Margaret nodded.

"And you said the four of you are doing it by that van. Christ, that'd take you forever. Miami waterfront is immense. All those little islands . . ."

Margaret put down her glass and reached into her handbag. "It's all we got. We'll give it a couple more days. Someone has to have heard of her." She plucked out a cigarette and after a little difficulty with the wind, got it lit. After taking a long puff, she stood up to go. "Well, thanks anyway."

"Just hold on a minute," Mrs. Manuzzi said, frowning. She took a quick glance at her husband, who nodded imperceptibly. "Bring your friends on board. We were just going out for what we call a little afternoon fun run. No reason why we old-timers shouldn't stick together in time of need."

Margaret was silent for a moment. "You mean that?" she finally managed.

"Absolutely," Mr. Manuzzi said. "We can cover ten times as much on the water as you can on land. Besides," he said, grinning, "we could use the company. Bring them on. There's plenty of room."

"Thanks a million," Margaret said. "I'll be right back. They won't believe this."

"No need to hurry," Mrs. Angelina Manuzzi called after her. "We can hit fifty knots . . . no problem."

CHAPTER 17

...

In less than twenty minutes, Margaret had heard the highlights of their life story since they were married. Carl had been a scrap metal dealer servicing the nonferrous foundries and sheet metal fabricators of North Jersey. In the forty years since he opened his door, he had saved enough to send his two daughters to college, set up a son-in-law in an accounting practice, buy a few trinkets for Angelina, and still have enough for the odd impulse purchase . . . like *The Mighty Moe*. Moe, it turned out, had been his business partner who, after thirty-five years of haggling over half cents per pound, had a stroke during the third round of the second Spinks/Ali fight. He never lived to see the stirring fifteenth round, much less enjoy the fruits of his many years of labor. Two months later Carl closed his doors, sold his equipment, and bade farewell to the scrap business. At the time he was sixty-seven, full of untapped energy, and had a strange yearning to be near the ocean.

Angelina, however, was no easy pushover. She had her friends, her family, her rituals, and they were all centered around Paterson. It took some skillful negotiating on Carl's part, but she finally settled for six months in Florida, six months in New Jersey, and a fifteen-carat, pear-shaped diamond brooch. That had been nine years earlier and neither had regretted the decision. Where else could you get great pastrami sandwiches, a terrific suntan, and nightly jai alai quinielas, all in the month of January.

The Mighty Moe came after they'd spent three years staring at Biscayne Bay from their third floor condo on

Stillwater Drive. Carl had never done anything in a timid fashion, so when it came to a choice between the Roballo and some floating excuse for a cocktail party, the speedboat won hands down. It never ceased to please them, either racing around the open waters west of Key Biscayne or poking around the little canals near Golden Beach. A couple of hours on board *The Mighty Moe* erased a week of land-based cobwebs.

Not so for Berdie who, after ten minutes bouncing on the choppy waters, retired below with a complexion that resembled the color and texture of newly skinned eggplant.

"Guess she's not used to all the movement," Angelina said. "She'll be okay when we slow down. Tomorrow she should have her sea legs."

"Tomorrow?" Margaret asked. "Certainly one day of your time is more than enough."

"Oh no," Carl said, working the controls. "This is more fun than watching a bunch of scrap dealers at a Chinese restaurant. We'll stick with it until we find her. *The Eternal Holidaze* can't stay hidden for long. Not with the Manuzzis on her case."

"Not to mention the Dream-trippers," Sid added, and settled back on the broad vinyl seat with a pair of binoculars.

"Where's this Forstman's anyway?" Angelina asked.

"Up on Bay Road, near Venetian Causeway," Durso said. "Maybe we should start there first."

"No," Carl said. "First we go see my buddy Pete Feezel, the smartest boat salesman in Florida. If anybody should know about a particular boat, he would. Besides, his school is right near Venetian."

"School?" Margaret asked. "For boat sellers?"

Carl laughed. "No, sales yard is on one side, ski school's on the other. As he likes to say, 'We show 'em and tow 'em.' Besides, Pete's one of us. If he's under seventy I'll eat my Medicare card."

"Well, okay," Margaret said, and hung on for dear life as the Roballo made a sharp turn around a channel marker.

■ ■ ■

Feezel's Ski School consisted of three fast Bayliner 2250s, a room full of skis, life jackets, and tow ropes, and two bronzed young men reading the latest copy of *Playboy*. Feezel, they said, could be found in the showroom down the dock. Carl flipped his bow rope to the taller one of the instructors, then did the stern line himself.

"Not too busy today, Nick?" he asked as he clambered on shore.

"Not today, Carl. 'Less some of your guests want to go," he added with a mischievous smile. "We got a special on parasailing this week. Twenty dollars over to Buena Vista and back."

Carl looked at the four New Yorkers who were struggling over the sides of his boat. "I don't think so," he said. "Watch her for me, will you. We'll be back in ten minutes." After they were all together he started down the dock toward his friend.

CHAPTER 18

...

Pete Feezel had enough lines in his face to justify his greeting Carl with a handshake and a "Hello there, young fella." The sun had not been kind to his exposed skin, but then people who spend most of their time outdoors enjoy other benefits. Feezel, wearing shorts and a shirt that had more colors in it than a Hawaiian sunset, looked as trim as one of his ski instructors. His crewcut also helped take off some of the years.

"What can I sell you today?" he asked with a broad smile.

"Some help," Carl said. "Let's go into your office, Pete. We gotta talk. These are my friends, Margaret Binton, Joe, Berdie, and Sid."

"Glad to meet you. Any friends of Carl and Angelina's are friends of mine and probably just as crazy. What's up?"

When they were inside the spare office, Margaret asked about *The Eternal Holidaze*. Pete scratched his stubbly head and squinted.

"Seems to me I've seen that boat, but damned if I can place it. Been down here long enough so's I should be able to know them all. Wait a minute . . . is it an old Trumpy . . . seventy-five feet, something like that?"

"We have no idea," Durso said. "Up until today we didn't even know it existed."

"Yeah, I think that's it. Can't be sure, of course, but that little foolishness about the 'daze' and 'days' seems to ring a bell. I think I seen it heading over to Sunset Isles . . . that area."

71

"Is that nearby?" Margaret asked.

"Not far," Pete said, "unless you're swimming. It's just on the other side of the causeway, maybe half a mile."

"And Forstman's?" Sid chimed in.

"Who?" Feezel said.

"Forstman's. It's an old age rest home on North Bay Road near Sunset Drive."

"Why yes," Pete said. "Then it's up in that area too. Only thing is there's four Sunset Isles. Plenty of dockage to put a large boat."

"That's where we come in," Carl said and turned toward the door. "Come on, we can be there in five minutes."

CHAPTER 19

...

Carl eased into the canal between West Twentieth and Twenty-first Streets doing no more than three knots. The waterway, about seventy-five yards wide, separated the mainland from the four small islands. The first of the Sunset Isles was on their left, North Bay Road on their right. Up ahead about two blocks they saw the back of Forstman's, and for the first time Margaret noticed it had a dock in back with a tiny boat tied up. Carl turned *The Mighty Moe* into the channel that separated the first two islands. Margaret watched as their stern swung out behind them and pointed to the guest house over a hundred yards away.

The motor of *The Mighty Moe* dropped a note as Carl worked the throttle back toward him. They were passing all sorts of pleasure boats on both sides as they headed up the channel.

"Anything?" he asked.

"Keep going," his wife said. "That's a good speed."

All of them were quiet now, watching as they passed boats no more than fifteen yards on either side of them. Even Berdie was on deck trying her best to help. Several times someone called out to slow or back up so they could check a name, but by the time they had weaved in and out of two more canals and were finishing up with the third island they were about ready to give up. Then Carl called out from his position at the controls, "Isn't that a Trumpy," and almost immediately Sid had the name.

"Get below," he called. "It's her."

Carl put it in neutral and everyone skittered down the

companionway. From below deck they could look out the three side port holes as they slowly pulled past her.

The Sequoia, the presidential yacht from Hoover through Ford, was a Trumpy design. But all the Trumpies, built in the thirties through the early seventies, were known for quality, elegance, and style. Their interiors were fitted out like corporate board rooms with carved ash, teak, and mahogany paneling, and in some cases cut glass window trim. They were the Rolls Royces of luxury wooden boats and still maintained their value in an age of fiberglass. This Trumpy, at seventy-five feet, was on the small side, but what it lacked in length, it certainly made up for in polish. Margaret had never seen such a beautiful boat. They were past in under a minute and made the turn out into the bay.

"Anybody see any activity?" Sid asked.

"Looked empty to me," Durso said. "Shades on the cabin were drawn. All the doors were closed. No wet bathing suits or towels drying. Don't think anyone's on her."

"Let's risk going around again," Margaret said. "I want to get a closer look. I also want to check how far it is by water from Forstman's. We'll stay below." She called up to Carl to double back and skim right past the Trumpy. Then she leaned against the bulkhead and concentrated on staring out the porthole.

This time when they cruised past, Carl kept it to a drift. Durso had called it accurately. There were no traces of anybody on board, which explained why the gangplank was drawn up. For all that, it was obvious that someone was taking good care of her. There were enough brass fittings topside to sink a lifeboat, and they were all gleaming in the late afternoon sun. Margaret looked toward North Bay Road and after a few seconds, found Forstman's. It was diagonally across the larger canal and perhaps two hundred meters away.

She turned away and called up to Carl. "Let's go. Not much more we can do here."

Immediately the engine took on a faster pitch and they started back toward the Venetian Causeway. When they cleared the last of the Sunset Isles, they all came on deck.

"Well, we found her," Sid said. "Now what?"

"Back home," Margaret said. "It's getting late. We'll figure out what to do over a nice dinner of spaghetti and meatballs. I don't know about you, but I can't think on an empty stomach."

"You're just lucky," Berdie said slowly. "You can even contemplate a full one."

CHAPTER 20

...

As much as they would have loved to sample Margaret's spaghetti and meatballs, Carl and Angelina begged off joining the dinner. They had tickets to hear Vic Damone and nothing short of a family crisis would keep Angelina from hearing her idol. Vic Damone had crooned on the radio of the old '47 Ford the night Carl had invited her on their first drive. And it was Vic Damone who signed his autograph the one and only time they flew first class to Florida. When she heard he was doing three nights at the Diplomat, she was at the box office a half hour before it opened. Italian food was Carl's favorite, but hey, Mr. D. himself . . .

She gave Margaret their address and phone number with strict instructions to call. The boat was available for whatever she had in mind, and so were they. A little adventure, Carl had said, was the best thing to make you feel young again. They dropped the four New Yorkers off and took a few minutes to close up their boat. By the time they stopped by the Winnebago to say good-bye, the drinks were poured and Margaret already had the meatballs in the oven.

■ ■ ■

When the dishes were all cleared away and the coffee was brewing on the stove, Margaret finally spread a map of Miami on the dinette. After studying it for a few moments, she put a mark over Forstman's and another over where *The Eternal Holidaze* was berthed. On the large map, the proximity of the two dots was suggestive enough.

"It seems to me we could take two approaches," Margaret began. "Straight surveillance, or some background investigation. Now that we know where the boat is, I suppose we could find out whose property it's on and what the connection is. But if Miami is anything like New York, and municipal files being what they are, I'd say it would be difficult to uncover anything concrete. I noticed the boat is registered in Delaware, probably for tax reasons, so we can't even trace it through the Florida Motor Vehicles Bureau. Anyone got a relative in Wilmington?"

The others shook their heads.

"So I guess I vote for surveillance," Margaret concluded. "Pure and simple. We've done it before, remember. And with this Winnebago, it'd be much easier. It means, of course, postponing the sightseeing trips for a while."

"We already decided on that," Durso said. "Frankly, I was getting a little tired of the Miami Seaquarium."

"So we'll keep an eye on Forstman's," Margaret said. "Keep an eye on the boat . . . see what develops. Mr. Schecter wouldn't have passed on his note unless there was some reason. Too bad we can't get anybody inside. That would be ideal, but Forstman said the place had no vacancies."

"What if nothing develops?" Durso asked with a note of skepticism in his voice.

"Something will develop," Margaret said. "Count on it."

CHAPTER 21

...

The next morning right after breakfast they attempted to buy a pair of binoculars. The problem was that they couldn't agree on what kind to buy. Sid wanted them to get a 7 X 30, the standard track binocular. Durso argued that a minitelescope with greater power would be preferable because they could see detail better (including some nearby planets, since astronomy was one of his hobbies). Berdie lobbied for little opera glasses that could be concealed better (and would fit snugly in her handbag whenever she went to concerts in Central Park). Margaret shook her head in disbelief.

"For God's sake," she groaned. "How are we going to pull this off if we can't even agree on the equipment? We need the Salt Two negotiators before we even get started."

They finally settled on a reasonable Japanese 8 X 21 wide-angle job that was both light and powerful. Then they headed in the direction of the Sunset Isle Canal. They found a little grove of trees by the water on Twenty-fifth Street and Margaret turned off the motor. The glasses enabled them to see perfectly any activity on board *The Eternal Holidaze* across the canal. Forstman's, however, was two blocks away and obscured around a little bend in the road.

"Joe, you take the first shift with the glasses," Margaret said. "Berdie, how about you taking a leisurely walk by Forstman's just to stretch your legs. See what you can see."

"What she's going to see is a perfectly pleasant exterior

to a perfectly normal-looking guest house," Durso said. "I can't imagine anything interesting will come of it."

"A little fresh air, at worst," Sid said. "Where's the harm? I think we're going to give you the pessimist of the month award."

"Mr. Rossman," Durso said without missing a beat, "go suck a lemon."

Sid grinned and sat back with the morning *Herald*. "Let me know when you need me," he said putting on his reading glasses. "I'll be in the sports section." He gave a little chuckle, but no one else found it particularly funny.

"Okay," Berdie said and got up. "I'll be back." She opened the door and shuffled out.

"I don't think her heart is in it," Durso said picking up the glasses. "Berdie never likes adventures . . . at least nothing stronger than the odd Lotto ticket."

"I suppose you do," Sid said flipping a page.

"From four hundred yards away . . ." He smiled and adjusted the focus. "I'm your man."

■ ■ ■

Berdie came back in forty minutes, ambling along at a slow pace with a seagull next to her. Every now and then Berdie flipped the bird a Ritz Cracker from her handbag. "My God," Sid complained. "She's hopeless."

"Anything?" Margaret asked when her friend was finally aboard.

"Nothing. The place was quiet. I thought it wouldn't do to just stand and stare, so I got me a cracker and in no time I had a friend. I spent about twenty minutes in front. Such a nice day and no one outside. They've still got the same NO VACANCY sign on the mailbox. I don't know where all the people are. The place gives me the creeps."

"That was clever with the bird," Margaret said, giving Sid a piercing stare. "We'll have to figure something out. I'd love to get inside again."

Durso put down the glasses and wiped his eyes with a handkerchief. He turned around toward the two women and shook his head.

"Also nothing here. No sign of anyone and not one boat gone anywhere near her."

"Maybe they only come on at night," Margaret said. "Why don't you take a break and let me look for a while."

Durso gladly handed over the binoculars and relinquished his place on the dinette next to the window. He rubbed his shoulders and his neck, and then lay down on the couch opposite.

Margaret raised the binoculars and started working with the focus. "My God, Joe, you're as blind as a bat. There, that's better." She settled down with her elbows on the table and remained motionless for almost a minute.

"Did you notice," she asked without lifting the glasses, "that there's someone on the next boat? An older man."

"Yeah, I saw him," Durso said.

"Well, I was just thinking . . . if boating etiquette is anything like suburban etiquette, that man will have had quite a few conversations with his neighbors. Equipment, boats, weather, stuff like that. Then again, he might have overheard something suspicious just being so close. It's worth a try. Maybe he'll be able to shed some light on things."

"How do you propose doing that?" Durso said sitting back.

"Simplest way I know. Just ask him." She bent down to put on her white, low-soled sneakers. "People are normally very friendly, especially with other old-timers. Watch." Without listening to Berdie's objections, she opened the door, dropped down to the pavement, and started walking to a nearby bridge that would take her to the last Sunset Isle.

"This I gotta see," Berdie said and grabbed the glasses. Durso lay back down on the couch and closed his eyes. Berdie looked for a few minutes but when Margaret went behind a row of houses, she lost her.

"Leave it to her to dive right in," Durso said, more to himself than to Berdie.

"Oh, there she is." Berdie rested the front of the binoculars against the window to steady them and watched as her friend advanced on *The Eternal Holidaze* and its neighbor. "Too bad we can't hear what she's saying."

■ ■ ■

Margaret advanced slowly down the grass strip next to the bulkhead until she came abreast of *The Eternal Holidaze*. The boat was just as beautifully maintained as it had appeared from the water. The teak trim had been carefully oiled, the brass recently polished, the windows were unsmudged, and the deck ropes all neatly coiled. The saloon windows were too darkly glazed for her to see inside, so she walked along the bulkhead toward the wheelhouse. Inside she spotted all sorts of expensive-looking equipment, which she guessed had something to do with the radar gizmo on the roof. She took a few steps further until she was standing abreast of the next boat's stern, a forty-foot fiberglass job called *Daddy's Toy*.

"What a beauty," she said loud enough for the older man sanding a rail down nearby to hear. "I bet she's a Trumpy."

"That's right, grandma, how'd you know?" He continued sanding, but his eyes were on her.

"Grandma . . ." Margaret smiled. "That's a laugh. Why, I bet I'm younger than you are."

"Maybe," he said. "Then again, maybe not." He leaned over the rail and squinted. To Margaret, he looked like the Puerto Rican handyman at the Florence E. Bliss Senior Citizens Center back in New York. The somewhat similar accent helped make the connection. He had a dark bushy mustache, salt and pepper curly hair, plenty of interesting creases around his eyes, and a nose that could have made its own slipstream. All in all, as faces go, it was pretty friendly.

"I know she's a Trumpy because I like boats, especially the old wooden ones. Looks like someone is taking good care of her." She let the statement hang there while she took a step closer to him.

"They do okay by her. When you have the kind of *plata* these boats cost, what's a few extra thou to keep them up. This boat here," he looked behind him, "is owned by some dentist from Cincinnati. Comes down only twice a year to do a little marlin fishing. Lets me live on it plus gives me fifty a week to keep it in shape. Can't beat that arrangement."

"No you can't," Margaret agreed. "But mind you, if I were doing it, I'd rather do it on a real boat," she nodded at *The Eternal Holidaze,* "one like that. She's got more romance in a single deckboard than that entire tub you're standing on." She winked at the older man. "Think they need an extra able-bodied cook?"

The workman shook his head and went back to sanding. "I don't think so. They seldom go out and you wouldn't like the company."

"How's that?"

"Bunch of *jefes grandes,* big shots. The owner rarely ever comes down. It's a shame they don't use her more."

"He must have a lot of money to burn." Margaret opened a fresh pack of Camels and reached over to offer one to the man. He stopped sanding and plucked one out. Margaret lit her own, then held the match for him. "What's he, a businessman or something?"

"Don't know. I never spoke two words to him." He inhaled deeply. "Damn, this tobacco is good. These days there's too many of these new sissy cigarettes around. Don't know whether to smoke them or use them for seasoning." He took another puff. "Of course nothing's like the real stuff. Pre-Castro."

"I figured you were Cuban," Margaret said.

"In Miami," the man said, smiling, "everyone's Cuban." He held out a hand. "Name's Alvarez, Renan Alvarez."

She took it. "Margaret Binton, by way of New York."

He picked up the sanding block again and started working the rail with long strokes. The brownish powder that came off swirled away in the light breeze.

"You do all the work on the boat?" Margaret asked.

"Yeah. Electric, mechanical, motors . . . I do it all."

"How about her?" Margaret nodded at the boat next to them.

Alvarez nodded. "The *Holidaze*? Good friend of mine. Except he don't live on her. Comes down twice a week, Monday and Friday. Name's Eduardo."

"And the rest of the time she's empty?"

"Who said that? Rest of the time there's this guy that stays on her . . . down below. But that's why I said you wouldn't like the company. Unfriendly as hell. I suppose he's a watchman because of the shoulder holster. But, hey, I don't say nothing. Not even to Eduardo."

"He on now?"

"Nope. Not between ten and about one. Afternoon he

goes out for a coupla hours." He looked at his watch. "Probably be back in a half hour. Hang around if you want to see one ugly hombre."

Margaret took a last puff of her cigarette and threw it in the water at her feet. She looked up at Renan and shook her head. "Nope. But I'd love to chat to the owner about the boat." She put on her friendliest smile. "You have any idea how I might be able to find him?"

"I can't tell you his name, because I don't know it. All I know is when he comes it's in this big Mercedes. Not much good that'll do you. Of course, there's always Eduardo."

"Your friend."

"Yeah. Would you believe it, we left Havana on the same ship . . . 1959. My best buddy. He would know. Come back on Friday."

Margaret's face fell. "Renan, at our age, two days could be a lifetime. You got any other ideas?"

"He lives pretty far out, way past the airport." He thought for a moment. "But I know where he hangs out almost every evening. It's right in Calle Ocho . . . little Havana, a cafe with a jukebox and the coldest *cervesas* in Florida. I could take you there." He threw his own butt in the water over the transom. "One thing, you gotta like *boliche* and *cuchi fritos*." A tight little smile creased his face.

"Hey, no problem," she said. "You're talking to a New Yorker here."

CHAPTER 22

...

Margaret adjusted the little woolen shawl she put on for the occasion and checked to see that her hair was still neatly coiled in the bun at the back of her head. She couldn't remember the last time she had been in a bar, especially with a man who was practically a stranger. She had no idea what the proper etiquette was. But now, as she looked at the Perro Negro Rinconica with its big yellow sign, Comidas and Criollas, she made a quick decision. A liberated gesture of paying for her own tab was best made over a lunch of quiche with her nephew. Drinking cold *cervesas* with a bunch of Cubans called for a more traditional approach. She followed politely behind Mr. Alvarez and smiled as he held the door for her.

Inside, the smell of stale smoke and damp bar rags was as heavy as the salsa coming from a juke box against the wall. The lighting was just the right level to cause severe eyestrain trying to read the one menu that hung above the bar. Margaret suspected that neither the patrons nor the cook paid much attention to it anyway. It was the kind of restaurant where people ordered what they felt like and the cook obliged. Which is to say that most everyone ordered *arroz con pollo* and left it at that. And Budweiser . . . in large cans that Margaret thought were only used for motor oil. Alvarez led them to a table by the bar and held out her chair. His eyes swept the room before he sat down next to her.

"He's not here yet," he said. "But we're early. Have a

drink while we wait. They got *fruto bomba, mamey, trigo . . .*"

"A beer would be fine," she said and lit up a cigarette. Her smoke swirled up to the ceiling and got lost in the layer that was already there. A waiter came over and Alvarez simply held up two fingers.

"This place isn't very busy for six o'clock," Margaret said. "But then again, I don't suppose they have an 'early-bird special.'" She looked around the room at the dozen people inside, all men. A few of them returned her glance, but then went back to their animated conversations. They all appeared to have just gotten off work. Sleeves on dirty shirts were rolled up, their hair was tousled, and their tired faces were never more than a few inches away from their cold beers. Every now and then one would burst into laughter, lean closer to a friend and share the joke. The words that drifted over to Margaret were in Spanish. She took another puff and watched as the waiter made his way over with the drinks. On the way he passed the only two pictures on the wall, a colorful mural of Jose Marti, and a black and white glossy of Alexis Arguello in his boxing gloves.

"Friendly place," she said. "How's the food?"

"Filling. Just stay away from the *bistec.*" Alvarez took a swallow of his Budweiser, wiped his lips, and moved closer. "You want to tell me what's so interesting about *The Eternal Holidaze* that brings you all the way out here?"

"I told you, simple love of old boats. There can't be more than a dozen Trumpies in all of Florida." Margaret took a sip of her drink and looked him straight in the eye. "I'm afraid that's the best I can do, for you and Eduardo."

"Hey, for me it's okay, I'm here, no? For Eduardo . . ." He raised his shoulders and in the same movement clinked glasses with her. "To lucky days."

Margaret took another swallow of the cold beer. Then Eduardo walked in and Alvarez motioned him over.

The first thing Margaret noticed was that Eduardo Diaz was short. He had a pleasant face with strong features crowned with a brush of white, close-cropped hair, all set on a body that could not have broken five-two. But unlike an Eddie Arcaro or Angel Cordero, Eduardo was a stocky little man with broad shoulders, the kind who could hold his own during a subway rush hour. He sat down with a grin in the chair Alvarez moved over for him.

"Renan," he said after the introductions were made, "you always surprising me, man."

"Yeah, well, Mrs. Binton here wanted to meet you. Something about that pile of kindling you work on."

"What about it?" he asked casually. But there was nothing casual about the look in his eyes.

"I'd like to talk to the owner," Margaret said. "I have a real interest in the old Trumpies, and when Mr. Alvarez said he knew you, why I thought I'd just ask."

"Course he knows me, I got him his job didn't I?" He looked over to his friend and grinned again. This time Margaret was close enough to see a gold tooth somewhere to the side of his mouth. "But the owner," Eduardo continued, "won't talk to you."

"Won't you let me try?" Margaret asked in her most grandmotherly voice. "What's the harm in telling me his name?"

"Because I give you his name and he finds out it was me, I might be out of a job."

Margaret sat back. "Eduardo, I'm too old to pester anyone. I get tired easily. I'm usually in bed by eight-thirty. If I got a 'no' on something I figure, so okay, finished. Now I just want to write him a simple letter with a few questions about the history of his boat. If he tells me he's not interested, fine, I won't do anything more." She took a deep breath. "And you know what, you don't even have to tell me. Write it on a piece of paper and just maybe it will drop out of your pocket. It's not your fault if they don't make pockets deep enough these days."

Eduardo's eyes narrowed, but slowly there appeared a tiny light of recognition in them. "So, lady, how deep are yours?"

Margaret leaned closer. "Deep enough to find a ten-dollar bill."

After a moment Eduardo turned to Alvarez. "She okay?"

Alvarez nodded. "I suppose so. Hell, what's it to you?"

Eduardo made up his mind. "Okay. You won't say where you got it?"

Margaret shook her head and fished around in her little change purse. In a few seconds she had the ten-dollar bill on the table before the other man.

Eduardo looked at it for a moment, then pulled a stub of pencil from his rumpled shirt and wrote something on the napkin. When he stuffed it into his pocket it was hanging halfway out.

"My lucky day," he said as he stood up and grabbed the ten. "See you around, Renan. If not at the pool hall, then on the dock." As he turned to leave, the napkin fell onto the floor. Margaret waited until he was halfway out the door before bending down to pick it up.

"Dr. Nelson Grimes?" she said slowly.

"Christ, the doctors got all the money." Alvarez raised his hand and motioned for the waiter. "Who do you think owns half the boats down here?"

But Margaret, lost in her own thoughts, didn't respond. The waiter approached and Alvarez indicated two more beers.

"And two *arroz con pollo*," he added.

Margaret was concentrating and didn't seem to have heard any of it.

"I wonder," she said softly, "if he's too busy to see a new patient."

"What?" Alvarez said.

Margaret looked up. "Oh, I just said at this hour I don't have too much patience. I hope they bring the chicken soon."

CHAPTER 23

...

Dr. Nelson Grimes was in the Miami phone directory. He had an office near the Heart Institute on Alton Road in a building that couldn't have been more than five years old. She gave her name to the receptionist in Dr. Grimes's quarters, was handed a preliminary form to fill out and asked to have a seat. The form was standard . . . identification, medical history, allergies, referred by, etc. Margaret filled in her name as Mabel Nussbaum, gave a fictitious address in New York, and scribbled in some other erroneous facts. She handed the paper back with a gracious little smile.

"Will it be a long wait?" she asked.

"Well, you didn't have an appointment," the young blond woman said frostily. "I'll see if the doctor can see you at all today."

Margaret sat back down and looked around her. There were four other patients waiting, all apparently over sixty-five and all looking quite glazed. Margaret leaned over to the nearest one.

"Excuse me," she said. "Do you know if Dr. Grimes specializes in anything else other than the . . . um, the . . ." she patted her midriff noncommittally.

"The heart?" her neighbor said, looking quizzically at Margaret's stomach. "No, just the heart."

Margaret leaned back. "Thank you so much." She turned her attention to the walls. Grimes's selection of art had a modern flair with a predominance of red swirls and rubbery-looking objects that could have been out of a medical text. She found more comfort in the three-month-old *Newsweek* on a table next to her and sat back for a long wait.

Grimes finally saw her two hours later. She was ushered into his presence by the nurse and cordially asked by the doctor himself to sit down. He was wearing an open white lab coat, but that was the only anonymous thing about him. His tie had a Countess Mara monogram to compete with the Oscar de la Renta initials on his shirt. His loafers had neat little Gucci buckles and his watch said Rolex. With all that Margaret would have expected Dunhill, but the brand of cigarettes he was smoking was Marlboro. She took it all in before answering his question.

"And Mrs. Nussbaum, how can I help you?"

"It's my heart," she said softly, touching her left chest. "I've never had a problem before, but now, in the middle of my trip, I'm getting little stabs out of it."

"You're on a trip? Does that mean you have no regular physician here in Miami?" He crushed his cigarette out in the full ashtray and leaned back.

Margaret nodded. "I called my doctor back in New York, Dr. Reynold. He's a GP, been my doctor for years. I guess he looked in a directory and told me to come here. I really don't think it's anything, but I did want to have it checked." She leaned forward. "Do you mind?" She touched his pack of cigarettes. "For later. I'm quite shameless when I run out."

"Well, I don't encourage it," Grimes said, "but as you can see I'm not a good role model. Help yourself. You were right to seek attention. Of course, the part that's over Medicare you'll cover by check."

"Of course." Margaret smiled. "I came on this trip with plenty of them."

"Fine. If you'll change into a gown next door, I'll see you in the examining room and have a look."

Two minutes later Margaret found herself on her back looking up at the cold end of a stethoscope.

"And what kind of trip are you on, Mrs. Nussbaum? Thinking of relocating to Florida?" While he spoke his hands kept moving the instrument across her chest.

"Oh no, not me. This is strictly a pleasure trip."

"You're going back up north?" he asked, frowning. "You're bucking the trend. We have so many fine places to stay here, from expensive condos to more reasonable guest hotels. And you can't beat the climate . . . turn over please."

Margaret rotated and put her head on her crossed hands. "I have too many friends up north . . . and a nephew I'd miss if I lived here all the time. But I certainly can see the appeal. That's why I brought Mr. Rossman with me. Man's all alone in the world. Just lost his wife last year, poor dear."

"He's looking to stay down here?"

"Uh-hunh," Margaret said as Dr. Grimes finished with her back and asked her to turn over again.

"This is an electrocardiogram. Ever had one before?"

"At seventy-two?"

"Then you know there's nothing to worry about."

During the few minutes it took him to put her on the machine he was too busy with the gel and suction cups to say anything. Finally he checked on all the leads and turned on the power. Margaret heard a little humming noise and out of a metal box came a strip of paper with some markings on it.

"No family down here or friends? How's he going to find a place?" Grimes picked up where he left off.

"I guess we'll just have to go from one apartment hotel

to another. I don't know . . . perhaps you could recommend someplace."

"Perhaps I could," he said and began to check her with some other instruments. "What . . . ah . . . what can he afford?"

"He's comfortable," she said. "Mind you, not one of the big hotels on the ocean. He's looking for a hotel where he can make some friends his own age."

"Which is?"

"Seventy-five. Least that's what he admits to."

Doctor Grimes didn't say anything for another several minutes while he went through the routine of checking Margaret's blood pressure, pulse, and other signs. At the end of it he shook his head.

"Mrs. Nussbaum, for a seventy-two-year-old lady, you're in terrific shape. I don't see anything wrong and the cardiogram doesn't indicate anything to worry about either. I could comment on your smoking, but then I don't really have a leg to stand on. Still, you should try to give them up. Maybe you'll have more success than I have. They'll probably kill me in the end. Now, I can do more extensive tests on your heart in the hospital, but that's up to you. I really don't see any need for it. But," he shrugged, "if the pains continue, come back." He brushed a speck of lint from his sleeve. "Now, while you're getting dressed I'll make a call. Turns out a good friend has a rest home right nearby. He usually doesn't have any vacancies, but, with a recommendation from me, he might find space."

"I'd really appreciate that," Margaret said, smiling. "And so would my friend. Between you and me, he's not a very assertive type and quite frankly I was worried he'd take the first place he went into and God only knows what that would have been like. When I tell him it's your recommendation, he'll be very happy."

"Mr. Rossman, you said."

"Yes, Sidney Rossman."

"He sounds like he'd fit in just fine. It's a quiet kind of place."

CHAPTER 24

...

Sid put up a little fight, but it was hopeless. When Margaret had something in mind, she was quite implacable. Someone who didn't know her so well would have argued for the better part of a morning and still given in. As it was, Sid had lost too many arguments to her to bother wasting both his time and energy. After a couple of unsuccessful ploys at diverting her, he finally nodded and agreed to become the "inside man."

"But what's my cover story?" he asked.

"Just be yourself . . . Mr. Sidney Rossman, from New York. I told Doctor Grimes you just lost your wife, but I don't think poor Emma would mind if we gave her a few extra posthumous years. You've decided to stay in Florida full-time and were looking for something small and friendly." Margaret lit a cigarette and watched the smoke for a moment. "God knows why, but I got the impression that he's looking for lost souls, and the closer you fit that the better."

"Hold on, just a minute," Sid said. "What good is this all going to do if I can't communicate with you. You said they were sticky about their guests leaving unattended."

Margaret thought for a minute. "Well, there's always your infirm old cousin from Sarasota whom you never see."

"My cousin?" Sid asked. "Who's that?"

Margaret pointed. "Mrs. B. Mangione, who'll make a sustained recovery a week after you arrive and come to visit one morning." There was a twinkle in her eye. "I think that'll do nicely. They wouldn't keep harmless old Berdie from seeing her cousin."

"I'm not going inside that place," Berdie said quickly.

"If Sid can do it for a week or so, you can do it for one morning. Besides, I'm not sure Sid'll be allowed to receive calls."

"What if things get rough?" Berdie said.

"We'll go to the police. If we get them some concrete information, they'll move. Joe, you'll be responsible for keeping an eye on the boat. We should be able to piece something together and give it to Diamond."

"So, once I'm in, what do I do?" Sid asked with resignation.

Margaret took another puff on the Camel and leaned heavily on the dinette table. "First of all you've got to speak to Schecter. Find out what he meant. And keep your eyes open. See if there's anything unusual for an old-age guest house."

Sid slapped his paper back open. "I sure hope they have a TV set. It could get pretty boring."

"They do," Durso said. "A big Sony in the living room."

"But boring"—Margaret shook her head—"is not exactly the word I would have used."

■ ■ ■

Early the next morning, two days after Margaret was ejected from Forstman's guest house, Sid found himself standing nervously in front of the man who had ordered her departure. However, this time, William Forstman couldn't have been more polite.

"Doctor Grimes mentioned you were coming," he said. "Also that you had no relatives in the area?"

"Not really," Sid answered. "There's an old cousin lives

near Sarasota, but she's not been too well lately. That's all. Friends are all dead except for Mrs. Nussbaum who is on her way back to New York."

Forstman nodded. "Medicines? You take anything special from a pharmacy?"

What a question. Sid thought. Everyone over sixty takes something even if it's only Maalox. "Nah. Maybe an aspirin or two."

"Our policy," Forstman continued, "is to keep all the medicines and make sure they are taken on schedule. I asked only because if you had something, you would have to give it to our dietician."

Sid shook his head.

"Well then," Forstman said after another moment. "As I told Doctor Grimes, I think we could fit you in. You are quite lucky, Mr. Rossman. We're very popular and we just now had an opening."

"Is that why the sign out front still says No Vacancy?"

"As you can see, we haven't even had a chance to change it." Forstman said without blinking. "Now, if you'll come back with your bags, the room will be ready. When you return, I'll explain some of the other house rules. They're strictly for the benefit of the guests . . . no loud noise, nothing to cause undue excitement, things like that. I'm sure you'll understand."

"Of course," Sid replied and shook Forstman's hand. "I'll be back in an hour. I'm looking forward to staying with you."

"You won't regret your decision," Forstman said. "No one ever has."

CHAPTER 25

...

By four that afternoon Sid had put all his clothes in the bureau, had a shave and a bath, and was ready for a little walk around the premises. It didn't take him long to discover that all the doors leading to the porches were locked. An attendant found him playing with one of the handles and stepped over. It was probably the same one Margaret had mentioned, because you don't find too many six-foot-two linebackers walking around in white coats. To Sid, whose movie-going had ceased after the courtship of his wife ended, the man looked like Hoot Gibson on steroids.

"They're all locked," the attendant said matter-of-factly. "Mr. Forstman wants to make sure the air-conditioning is kept at a comfortable level. Someone was always leaving a door open."

"Oh," Sid said and took a step back. "How do you get out on the porch?"

"We all go out from ten to eleven in the morning, and then again at two in the afternoon. I'm sure you'll find that more than enough fresh air." He stuck his hand out. "You're the new guest. My name is Franco. You'll be seeing a lot of me."

Sid shook his hand and immediately regretted it. It was obvious that Franco was making a point. When Sid pulled his hand back it felt more like chopped sirloin than something that once was able to hold a pencil.

"Welcome. If you ever need anything, let me know. I'm not hard to find. I kinda roam around."

Epsom salts for a start, Sid thought, but just smiled. "When's dinner?" he asked.

"Five-thirty to six-fifteen." Franco looked at his watch. "Plenty of time still for you to play some cards or watch the news."

"I think I'll just wander around . . . get to look at my new surroundings," Sid said. "Was that a boat I saw out back?"

Franco nodded. "It's just a little pedal boat we take out for exercise. I try to go every day with someone else. It's great for the circulation."

"I'd like to try it sometime."

"Sure, soon as I get an opening, we'll go out." He gave Sid a friendly sledgehammer pat on his shoulder and turned to go. "See you later. Glad to have you aboard."

"Likewise I'm sure," Sid said softly to himself and turned in the opposite direction.

As far as he could tell, there wasn't too much room downstairs for wandering. There was the large living room with the television set and a dozen or so places to sit, the dining room with four tables seating sixteen, Forstman's office, a bathroom, and a card/game room. However, the rooms were spacious and the ceilings high enough so that claustrophobia was not an immediate threat . . . at least not for someone who had been there for only two hours. Sid wasn't sure how he'd feel after a few days, with the locked doors.

"Hello, you the new one?"

Sid turned and saw an old woman beside him. She was leaning on a cane and peering closely at him. Sid estimated that she had at least ten years on him if not more, which was perhaps why her clothes hung a little too loosely from her shoulders.

"News travels fast around here," Sid said. "I just got here a few hours ago."

"My name's Josie Epping. Been here five years." She straightened up a little and leaned closer. "How long you in for?"

Sid couldn't help but laugh. "Ten to twenty on aggravated assault."

"And a sense of humor, no less. Come, let's sit down and talk. You're the first new person we've had around here in months."

Sid waded right in. "What happened to the last one?"

"Mr. Schecter." She sighed and slowly made it to a seat in the living room. "I thought you knew. It's his room you got. Poor man died day before last. Ambulance took him out around midnight."

Sid felt the blood drain from his face. He hoped it wasn't too noticeable but he felt as though the floor had just disappeared.

"What happened?" he finally managed.

"They told us it was a heart attack," she said simply. "Found him in his room when he didn't show for dinner. Terrible shame, he was such a nice man." She looked up at Sid, who had regained some of his color. "But in a place like this, death is at your elbow all the time. We learn to live with it like a lingering toothache. One goes out, another comes in. But then I don't suppose I'm telling you anything new."

"Oh no," Sid said slowly. "I'm rather speechless."

CHAPTER 26

...

It was after ten-thirty when Sid ventured out of his room. He figured that by that time all the other guests would be asleep and Franco or whoever was on duty would be settled comfortably in front of the television. But Sid had his story ready. Old-timers were always getting up to go to the bathroom or for a midnight walk, just as he was doing this first night in a strange bed. If anyone caught him he would say he was trying to walk himself to sleep. He crept down the corridor, hesitating at each open door, until he got to the staircase. A light was burning downstairs in the office. He went down as slowly as he could, holding his breath at the bottom. He could hear the muffled noise of a television coming from the office as he slowly slipped around the banister and through the door of the kitchen.

He had only a confused notion of what he was looking for. Above all he wasn't even sure that Schecter had been the victim of foul play rather than a bad heart. After all, he told himself, just like the lady said, old people are dying all the time. But something in his fine Yiddishe kop told him it was a crock and that the plug had been pulled on Schecter as surely as his name was Sidney Rossman, Ralph and Sadie's little boy.

The light in the kitchen, as in the hallways, was so dim he found himself nearly tripping over a stepstool stored against the wall. "Damn!" Sid grunted. "I'd like to see Margaret just once be the inside man. Ouch!" This time Sid bumped smack up against a stainless steel table. He grabbed the edge to keep himself steady as the pain in his shin slowly subsided. He listened, but the only noise was a steady hum coming from the refrigerator motor. After another minute he moved again. By now his eyes were getting used to the darkness.

The kitchen at Forstman's was larger than Sid expected. All the appliances appeared to be modern and the surfaces were all either Formica or stainless steel. There was one large preparation table in the middle of the floor, which effectively divided the kitchen in two. Storage was on one side, cooking on the other. There was a look of efficiency about the setup that Sid had noticed in the evening meal: The tomato juice had been exactly the same height in all the glasses, the chicken leg precisely centered on the plate between the perfect scoop of mashed potatoes and three-layered beets. Whoever ran the kitchen, Sid suspected, must have interned in an officers' mess. But Sid wasn't interested in checking out the culinary capabilities of Forstman's this evening, he was looking for the dietician's station . . . the place where the pills were dispensed.

In one corner of the kitchen was a Formica desk with a set of cabinets overhead. Unlike the other cabinets, these were locked with a heavy padlock. Sid slipped in behind the desk, and, keeping as low in the chair as he could, opened the top drawer. He had no idea what he was looking for, but began rummaging inside. Pens, paper clips, blank prescription forms . . . was there a doctor on staff? He reached in further and his hand came across a large notebook. Quietly he drew it out and opened it.

Whoever was keeping the records in the book had the same meticulousness that Sid saw around him in the kitchen. Each page was devoted to one guest and across the top were the names of the different pills they were taking. Then, in long columns underneath, were written the dates and the number of pills dispensed. Page after page of numbers. The listings of the drugs were varied. There was a lot of diazepam, Halcion, Tylenol #3, and Dyazide, but another drug cropped up a lot, something called Amobarbital. Sid also saw some insulin and Micronase for the diabetics, as well as heart medications like Inderal. There were others he had never heard of, and under each, a precise tabulation. He turned the pages towards the back and found Schecter's name. A big red line ran diagonally across the page but it didn't keep Sid from seeing a history of his medication. There wasn't much, just the diuretic, Dyazide, and Tagamet for ulcers, and Entex, an antihistamine probably for an allergy. That was interesting: Schecter did not appear to have had a heart problem. Sid ran his fingers down the column. Daily, Schecter had taken one Tagamet tablet, two Dyazide capsules, and a couple of Entex tablets, up until the day he died. Nothing suspicious there. Sid flipped back through the pages and looked at each of the other guests again. The dates under the columns flowed in a mostly unbroken rhythm. Here and there one of the people went without a pill, but at the most it was only for one day. Very rarely, in fact in only two instances, did anyone get more than his or her normal dosage. Sid noticed that both a Mr. Griswold and a Mrs. Young had been given four capsules of fifty-milligram Amobarbital just two days earlier, then they went back again to their normal two capsule dosage the day after. Sid looked up at the cabinet where all the medicines were presumably kept. When you stopped and thought about it, it was certainly a strange arrangement. Sid closed the book slowly. Efficient or not, whoever heard of a dietician or cook dispensing pills like a hospital doctor? Sid was sliding the book back when he heard the scuffing of footsteps outside the kitchen door.

"Christ," he said softly and sank down under the desk. He didn't even have a chance to close the drawer before the door opened and the lights were turned on. This is it, he thought. There was no way he could stretch a midnight walk to cover having his nose in someone's private desk. His heart was racing faster than it ever had on the handball court at the YMCA, and for one brief moment, he thought he'd pass out. But it didn't take him long to realize that whoever had entered the kitchen had just as quickly exited, but through a door on a different wall. Sid heard the sound of footsteps descending a staircase. He very carefully closed the drawer and after another minute poked his eye over the edge of the desk. The kitchen was indeed empty. The door to the cellar lay partly ajar but far enough away that he didn't have to cross it to get back to the hallway. The hell, he thought, I'm not waiting. He tiptoed around the stainless steel center table and slipped back out of the door. The television was now off, and as far as Sid could judge, the office empty. He risked it and walked straight to the foot of the staircase and started up. No one called him back or grabbed him around the throat. His hand on the banister was shaking and there was an unnatural tightness in his knees, but in another minute he was in his own room with the door closed. He just sat on his bed and waited until his pulse returned to normal. When it finally did, he turned his attention to the question he'd stuffed away in the frightened recesses of his brain the moment the cellar door opened: "Why in God's name would anyone use ether in an old age home?"

CHAPTER 27

...

Margaret pulled her heavy sweater out of the cabinet beneath the double bed and put it over her shoulders. The weather this morning, even by New York standards, was miserable. A steady rain was falling and gusts of cold wind rippled the surface of the water in the canal in front of them.

"Who said this was such a delightful climate," she asked, "you or Sid?"

Durso, who was looking at the boat through the binoculars, just grunted.

"Florida in November is no bargain," Margaret continued. "Travel agents and real estate brokers notwithstanding. Can you see anything?"

"Not yet, but it's early. You think Sid's all right?"

Birdie, sitting at the dinette table, put her coffee cup down a little too quickly and spilled some of the liquid. "I'm sure he is," she said abruptly. "No need to worry about Sid." She brushed a straggly lock of hair to the side of her forehead and picked up her cup again. "Right, Margaret?" Her eyes searched her friend's face.

Margaret nodded and touched the wiper button to clear the windshield. "I'm sure he's okay. In a few days you'll go in and visit, don't worry."

"Hey," Durso said softly, "there's that boat again."

The two women looked across the water and saw a sleek motorboat with blue lightning bolts painted on its sides cruise slowly into the canal.

"This is the second time he's been by in an hour,"

105

Durso said. "Doesn't stop, just goes through the canal slowly."

"Let me see," Margaret said, and reached out for the binoculars. Looking through a wet pane of glass and over 100 yards of downpour it was difficult for her to get a clear picture, but she thought she could see two men under the cockpit canopy of the speedboat. The boat was in the middle of the channel, but as it approached *The Eternal Holidaze* it slowly started to veer toward it.

"We may have something," Margaret said excitedly. "Hold on." She tried to get the name on its stern.

The speedboat stopped about ten feet away from the Trumpy but left its motor running. Then slowly, while Margaret watched, it backed a few feet and angled a little outward. Out of the corner of her eye, Margaret thought she saw a flashlight go on in one of the rear cabins of the Trumpy. When she looked closer, the window was blank.

"What's happening?" Durso asked. "I can't see anything."

"Nothing. The speedboat is just sitting there. No one's on deck. Did you see a light flash on in the Trumpy?"

Both Berdie and Durso said "No" at the same time. Am I seeing things? Margaret wondered. She kept watching but the scene didn't change. Then after about two minutes, the speed boat pulled away as smoothly as it had arrived. On the back she saw the name *Sea-ducer*. "Another wit," she mumbled, and handed the glasses back to Durso.

"So?" he said. "Something I missed?"

Margaret rubbed her eyes. "Nothing happened. He just backed up and turned a little, and that's all."

"Maybe they decided to cancel whatever they were going to do," Berdie said, "because of all the rain. If you ask me, though, I can't see as how a little water ever hurt anything."

Margaret grabbed the glasses from Durso again and quickly looked over at the Trumpy. "Berdie, I think that's it," she said.

"What's it?" Berdie looked perplexed.

"Drugs," Margaret said. "I think we just saw a delivery . . . underwater. Come on, they're heading north. We might just be in luck."

"You gonna chase them in a Winnebago?" Durso looked skeptical.

Margaret gunned the engine in reverse. "Very funny. Let's just hope Carl is by his phone."

CHAPTER 28

...

"Not going out today?" Sid asked Franco as he passed him in the living room. "I mean in the pedal boat. Weather's too rotten?"

"Probably clear up after lunch. Besides we have ponchos. There's always someone wants to go."

No doubt, Sid thought. Anything to get out of these claustrophobic rooms. He had spent the entire morning watching television with most of the other guests, as boring and docile a group as he had ever encountered. All his attempts at conversation had been met with perfunctory replies. Perhaps competing with a $25,000 pyramid was a losing proposition to begin with. He never could understand why old people liked watching young people win money. If he had his way it would be the other way around. He was counting on at least a half hour of undivided attention at lunch.

By pure coincidence he was seated at a table with Mrs. Epping and two others, a Mrs. Kass and Henry Griswold. Mrs. Epping introduced Sid to the others.

"Isn't this weather something," Sid began. "I was hoping to go for a walk around the grounds this afternoon."

"Not today," Mrs. Epping said. "It will never clear up in time for the afternoon walk."

"The afternoon walk?" Sid repeated.

"Yes, at two o'clock. Everyone goes out back at that time for an hour. The sun shines down just perfectly on the little area where the lawn chairs are."

"What if you wanted to go when the sun wasn't so perfect, say at one-thirty?" He started to raise a spoonful of soup.

"Oh," Mrs. Kass replied. "That wouldn't be possible. No, at one-thirty Shadow is out."

Sid just managed to get the spoon to his lips when he stopped. "So, what's wrong with a little shade?"

"Oh, Mr. Rossman, you don't understand," Mrs. Kass twittered. "Shadow is a black German shepherd they keep out back to protect us. Mr. Forstman is always telling us about the many burglaries that occur at other guest houses without dogs. We haven't had one here yet." She smiled and turned to Mr. Griswold. "Isn't that right?"

Griswold didn't seem to be the talkative type. He had an unchanging expression on his face that looked as if he was in a room full of dead fish. His mouth had little supporting it from the inside, the result of too many visits from the tooth fairy in his declining years.

"That's right," he offered and ladled some soup into his mouth.

"Well, how about the front then?" Sid asked. "Can you go for a walk there?"

"You've got to be kidding," Mrs. Epping chirped. "Against the rules. They don't have enough staff to keep an eye on everyone. Seems they lost one of the guests a while back. He just went out the door and disappeared. When dinner time came they noticed the empty seat and sent out the scouting party." She chuckled. "The way Mr. Forstman tells it, they found him way over on Prairie Avenue looking in a pet store. Man was slightly off his rocker. Now they keep the doors closed so it won't happen again."

"And to save on the air-conditioning," Mrs. Kass supplied.

"What if it did happen?" Sid asked casually.

"Oh God!" Mrs. Epping raised her eyes. "Stage one of the D code."

"Excuse me?" Sid said.

"The D code. It's their little system of discipline. Every organization must have its rules, Mr. Rossman. Haven't they told you yet?"

Sid shook his head. "And stage one . . ."

"No television for a day," Mrs. Kass interjected. "That's an easy one."

"There's a stage two?" Sid asked tentatively.

"No dinner. The number of days depends on how bad a thing you did."

"Stage three?" Sid asked leaning forward. He wasn't quite believing his ears.

"Yes, that's for the worst offenses," Mrs. Kass said. "Like for unauthorized phone calls, sneaking around at night, and especially for talking back to Franco or Mr. Forstman." She shook her head. "But they seldom have to use it. Everyone around here is very cooperative."

"What . . . um . . . happens?"

Mrs. Kass smiled, took another taste of her soup, and said quite simply, "No medication."

There was silence at the table for a few seconds. "Isn't that dangerous?" Sid finally asked, his eyes as big as nickels.

"Like Mrs. Kass said," Griswold interrupted, "it rarely happens. Besides, they only hold back the Valium or Seconal, not the important things."

Not so rarely, Sid thought, remembering the empty spaces in the medication book he had seen.

"And you don't find this system a little bit much?" Sid asked incredulously. "You don't mind?"

"Mind?" Mrs. Kass said in surprise. "No, why should we? They take good care of us here. The place is spotless, the food's good, and they are very conscientious about our pills. No one ever has to worry he'll forget to take something because they're always on a little tray waiting for us in our rooms. Like clockwork, always the same."

Sid looked directly at Henry Griswold. "They never make mistakes, like giving you the wrong pills or the wrong amount?"

Griswold raised his head and his eyes met Sid's. "Never happens. I've been taking two capsules of Amobarbital every day since I got here. They got a book or something. We don't even have to reorder. They do it for us."

Sid thought for a moment. "What exactly is Amobarbital?"

"Just a pretty strong sedative."

"Which means," Sid thought out loud, "if someone who wasn't used to them took four by mistake . . ." but Sid wasn't thinking mistake, he was thinking how easy it would be to switch powders inside capsule jackets " . . . and they had a glass of bedtime sherry afterwards, it might be a problem?"

Griswold laughed. "Hell, not after that," he said. "He'd just be dead."

Stage four of the D code, Sid thought angrily.

■ ■ ■

After the chicken soup came the frankfurters, thin, perfectly shaped rods of a meatlike substance that looked more bleached than cooked. They rested in the middle of all the plates, keeping in check the opposing forces of creamed corn and applesauce. A plate of white bread was put in the middle of the table to complete the meal.

"See, what'd I tell you," Mrs. Kass said, digging into her applesauce. "The food's good and healthy."

"Didn't you ever hear of linguini and clam sauce," Sid

grumbled, and stabbed the purported meat. His fork glanced off and the little slippery hot dog jumped halfway off the plate.

"Mr. Rossman," Sid heard over his shoulder and turned to see a woman in a kitchen apron. The resemblance to Betty Crocker stopped right there. The apron was as inappropriate on her as a pair of spike heels on Billy Jean King. Her teased red hair framed a face that had been outlined, highlighted, shadowed, rouged, blushed, mascaraed, and lipsticked by a myriad of products. The hand behind this art project seemed to have a measure of subtlety, but the outcome, nonetheless, was a little startling. "I'm Donna Slater," she said.

Sid nodded and pushed his frankfurter discreetly back into the center of his plate.

"I'm the dietician. I make up all the menus for our guests. Since you're new here, I came over to ask you some questions."

"Like what?" Sid asked.

"Do you have any special allergies or diets I should know about? Many of our guests have to have their food separately prepared."

Sid took a forkful of creamed corn. "Yes, come to think of it I do. I can't eat anything soft." He looked at her without flinching. "It's a special condition. Has something to do with infection of the gums."

"This is not a game, Mr. Rossman, I have a job to do. Anything you're not supposed to eat."

He shook his head. "There are some things I don't like, though." He took a glance down at his plate.

"Well, we all have our little idiosyncrasies now, don't we. I'm glad to see you won't be a problem." She made a note in a little pad she flipped open. "Now, about medications. I understand from Mr. Forstman that you are not currently taking anything."

"That's right, not currently nor in the foreseeable future."

"Well, in case you find yourself in need of a sleeping pill or a mild sedative—for whatever reason—we have a supply of things in my office. Just ask Mr. Forstman or Franco."

"Mild, nonprescription things you mean?"

"Yes, of course. But in case you need anything a little stronger, we can probably find you something."

I'll bet, Sid thought. Like Amobarbital, whatever that is. "Doesn't that require a prescription?" he asked, probing just a little further.

"Yes, of course." She laughed. "What do you think, Mr. Rossman, we're in the wholesale drug business? We have a doctor on call here and he approves all our medications. Think about it," she said, "in case you find it hard to go to sleep in new surroundings." She turned and headed for the kitchen. Sid watched her go before turning back to his lunch mates.

"You shouldn't kid her too much," Mrs. Kass said. "She can make things uncomfortable."

Sid was surprised. "I thought you said you were delighted with everything."

"Well," the other woman said, looking quickly in the direction of the kitchen door, "I'm not one to complain, but some things fall under the heading of necessary evils."

There was an awkward silence at the table for a moment.

"You know," Sid finally said, "it seems to me that you're all kind of locked in here, no matter what the explanations are. Locked up and maybe a little bullied. Doesn't anybody ever complain?"

"Sure," Mrs. Epping said, and straightened up. "Mr. Schecter was talking about it all the time."

CHAPTER 29

...

After lunch everyone went upstairs for a nap. Sid didn't particularly feel like a nap, but since there was no one else around to talk to, he decided to go up to his room and piece things together. It had only been a day since he arrived, but already he felt he had uncovered a lot. Of course he couldn't be sure about Schecter and Griswold's pills and there probably would be no way to check. Mrs. Epping was right. People were dying all the time in old-age homes and Schecter's demise was probably treated as routinely as all the others. The doctor of the guest house says he died of a heart attack, well then, who's to say he didn't. A neat little system, especially when the doctor in question is a friend of the owner.

Sid closed the door to his room and looked around. He walked absently to the bureau to close the top drawer, then hesitated. What registered was that one of his socks was lying on top of his undershirts. With a frown he pulled the drawer out and looked inside. As he did so, he remembered with sudden anger that the last thing he had done that morning before leaving the room was to close all the drawers tight. It was an old habit of his, as persistent as his fussiness in keeping his socks separated from his underclothes. Now, as he looked, he realized that someone else had been rummaging in his bureau this morning.

This is unreal, Sid thought and slammed the drawer shut. He checked the other drawers and his closet but there didn't seem to be anything missing.

"A goddamn spy novel," he mumbled. "People searching through your things when you're not there." He walked over to the window to look out. This place is dangerous, he thought. It was one thing trying to get some information out of people, maybe snoop around a little bit in the process. It was quite another when you became the target yourself. The hell with a couple of weeks, Sid thought, I'm getting out the day Berdie comes. He looked at the gray clouds scuttling by, and then down at the ground. The rain had stopped, but he could tell that it was still pretty windy and damp out. His room was in the back corner and faced both the canal and the side driveway. Across the driveway was a stockade fence and on the other side of that was a lawn and presumably another house. The fence, he guessed, was to keep Shadow from feasting on some of the neighbors.

Out of the corner of his eye he saw something move and looked up. At the little dock Franco and one of the guests were just getting into the yellow fiberglass pedal boat. Sid watched as they both settled into their seats, made a lazy arc into the canal, then headed to the right. The older man was doing some of the pedaling but didn't seem to be too happy to be out on the water. To Sid, however, it seemed like the perfect exercise. When you got tired you just took your feet away and Franco did all the work. The canal was protected so the water never got too rough and the whole time you were out of doors in the fresh air.

As he watched he noticed the little boat was making steady progress up the canal. It continued straight, splashing water out the back as its paddle wheels chugged along. It passed about ten feet away from the Trumpy but didn't stop. After going another thirty or forty yards it slowly started turning back. Both of its occupants were pedaling, although Franco seemed to be the one steering. Sid continued watching until the boat came full circle and landed back again at the guest house's little dock. The entire round trip had taken no more than fifteen minutes. Franco tied up the boat and helped his charge step out. Then, as the two of them walked toward the back door, Franco stopped and released a little gate. Sid saw a blur of black as the German shepherd bounded out and raced toward the water. When he got to the dock he turned and sat like a polite little house dog. But Sid wasn't buying it. Shadow had a purpose in life and it wasn't to be cute. Also, from the looks of it, his movements had been choreographed.

Sid turned away with a sinking feeling in his stomach. He hated dogs, especially the big kind. But his next move was obvious.

CHAPTER 30

...

"To the left," Margaret shouted. "I think they went in there."

Carl spun the wheel around and the big, double-engined Roballo responded in an instant. They were just approaching the Bay Harbor Islands and still on the trail of *Sea-ducer*. Fortunately Carl had been home when Margaret called breathlessly, and he made the ten blocks to his boat at the same time the Winnebago did. It had taken Carl only a few moments to rev up *The Mighty Moe* and cast off. *Sea-ducer*, unaware that anything was amiss, was tooling quietly north. Margaret thought she spotted it through the binoculars maybe a mile ahead of them when Carl finally got his boat out into the bay. Fortunately there were not many other vessels out in the ugly weather.

It had taken them fifteen minutes to catch up to within a few hundred yards, at which point Margaret spotted the name and smiled. "Keep a little distance back," she cautioned. A minute later, the driver of the other boat made a turn to the left and disappeared behind the Broad Causeway leading to Ninety-sixth Street. Shortly afterward Margaret shouted her directions.

"Left," she repeated again.

They made the turn under the bridge and just caught sight of *Sea-ducer*'s stern as it angled into one of the narrow canals that cut into the land.

"You want speed?" Carl asked but Margaret shook her head.

117

"I don't think he noticed us. Just go in slowly after him."

Carl's hand was itching on the throttle, but he did as Margaret wanted and took another three minutes to get to the spot where *Sea-ducer* had disappeared. They entered the narrow canal expecting to see him tying up or cruising slowly at its further end. They didn't expect to see a lifeless expanse of water with no less than two exit canals leading out in different directions.

Carl slapped the panel in front of him. "I should'a remembered this area of Arch Creek is a maze of canals. If we don't hurry he'll give us the slip." He glanced quickly at Margaret and she nodded. Carl hit the chrome handles a fraction of an inch forward and the Roballo jumped ahead. The end of the canal was no more than a couple of hundred yards away, but they made it there in less time than it took Berdie to holler and grasp her way below. Carl swung the wheel to the right and *The Mighty Moe* made a turn that just grazed a little catboat tied up at the corner. The stern wave the big Roballo created slapped up the bulkheads behind them, bouncing the moored boats on both sides off their poles. One of the many signs that said "No Wake, 4 MPH" was ripped off its post.

"It's a crapshoot," Carl yelled, looking ahead into yet another still canal. "But I'm going to keep heading north. Was the way he was headed." He spun the wheel again and slipped into another canal. The clearance in this one was no more than ten feet on either side, but Carl didn't touch the throttle. He was doing over fifteen miles an hour, but in the narrow passage it seemed as if he was flying. "Keep an eye out in case he's moored."

"I'm trying to," Margaret yelled, "but you're going too fast. Joe, you take the right side."

Durso nodded and stuck his head near the edge.

Carl zigged left into another canal, then right, then threw the throttle back into neutral as a little sixteen-footer started backing out from its space. He gave it a shot from his horn and managed to coax it back into its slip just as their momentum carried them past.

"Haven't had so much fun since we did the Bermuda run," he said, and threw the throttles back up. "Boy will Angelina be sorry she was out getting her hair done."

"Good lord," Margaret said, gripping onto a side rail in terror. "You think this is fun." She watched for a moment as he adjusted the controls, then went back to looking at the boats they were whizzing past.

Carl handled the boat well, but with each empty canal he pushed the Robalo a little closer to the edge. Finally, as they skittered around a tight little turn and into their eighth and what looked like the last canal before the bay, Margaret heard a thud and then a splintering sound beneath her. She was thrown to the side and barely managed to keep her hold on the rail. Carl cursed and pulled back on the throttle.

"I thought I had that one," he mumbled and leaned over the edge. He stayed that way for a few seconds while the boat glided to a stop in the water. When he pulled his head back he didn't look happy.

"The side's holed. Fortunately it's above the water line if I don't plane." He sat back down heavily in the control seat. "I'm afraid we're out of commission." He shrugged. "Well hell, we gave it our best. Son of a bitch must'a gone south." He advanced the throttle just slightly and the big boat started forward again, this time at something like a creep.

"Sorry," he added, "it'll take us a while to get back at this speed."

Margaret, who was looking out forward, nodded her agreement.

"Longer than you think," she said and pointed. "Isn't that a police launch coming this way?"

CHAPTER 31

...

Sid shifted nervously from foot to foot as he waited outside the kitchen door. Finally Donna Slater made her appearance.

"I'm sorry it took so long, but right before meals is my busiest time." She looked at him and waited. "You wanted something?"

"This afternoon at lunch you asked if I needed some medication to help me go to sleep. I'm sorry if I was a little quick to reply. I'm not used to drugs and they make me nervous."

"Yes?" Ms. Slater looked impatient.

"Well, I usually take a nap in the afternoon, but today I had a hell of a time getting to sleep. So I was wondering, maybe I should take you up on getting something for tonight. Come to think of it, I was up half of last night too."

Slater threw off a quick smile and nodded. "Certainly. You want something that'll just make you relax, or something stronger, something that'll knock you right out?"

Sid shrugged. "Why don't you give me one of each." He smiled innocently. "If the mild one doesn't work, I'll take the other one."

"No problem," she said and reached behind her for the door. "You'll find them on your night table tonight. They'll be clearly marked."

"Thank you," Sid said and started to turn away. "Oh, by the way, what's for dinner?"

"Salisbury steak," she said, "and lima beans."

"Perfect," Sid said and swung around. "My favorite."

■ ■ ■

"What's the matter, Mr. Rossman," Mrs. Epping asked at dinner. "You don't like Salisbury steak?"

He looked down at his plate where the round patty was sitting all by itself. "I'll get to it," he said and reached for another slice of bread. "But do I love limas. My wife Emma used to make them in a bacon butter sauce that put the finest restaurants to shame." He took a bite of the bread, then put it down on his plate, partially covering the meat. "Poor woman was the best cook in the world." He waited until the three others at his table were not looking, then swept the bread toward him. The meat slipped onto the waiting napkin in his lap. After a minute he put his fork down on the plate noisily and sat back. "Now, what do you think the dessert is?"

■ ■ ■

Opening the capsules to get the powder out was no problem. Getting it inside without crumbling the meat was another matter. In the end Sid found himself mixing everything together, then pressing the meat into a ball in the corner of one of the plastic wastebasket liners. He cut the plastic with about an inch overhang then tied the little bag loosely with a thin piece of string. The last thing he did was put a few small holes through the plastic so the smell would leak out.

He waited until midnight this time, long after he thought anyone was up and watching. After his eyes adjusted to the gloom of the backyard, he spotted faithful Shadow lying in his place in front of the dock. Carefully he opened the window as far as it would go, pulled the curtains to the side, and took a step back. He swung his arm in a side-arm motion, the same as his put-away handball shot, and the little bag flew dead center through the open window. It sailed out in a lovely arc, landed in the soft grass a few feet in front of the dog, and bounced twice. A perfect strike. Sid went back to the window and watched.

Perhaps Shadow had been trained not to take food from strangers. But a package of delicious-smelling meat that seemed to sail down from the trees didn't fit any scenario he had been walked through. He let out a little growl, looked around suspiciously, smelled the air, then waited. The package didn't move, there was nobody around, and there was this odor . . . after a minute, he got up and crept forward. He only had to go a few steps to get a closer look.

Sid waited impatiently. He saw Shadow push the little package with his nose, inspecting its underside. The dog gave one more quick look around, put a paw on the package, and tore into it with his muscular jaw. One minute it was there, the next it was gone. Sid looked for the telltale plastic on the ground but there was no sign of it. He turned away from the window and went back to his bed. He set his watch for one-thirty and closed his eyes.

The alarm woke Sid up from a recurrent dream about his favorite moment in life since the day he met Emma at an ILGWU picnic. The backdrop was the YMCA gymnasium on West Sixty-third Street. Sid was wearing his gym clothes and crouched low to put a handball in play. Joe Reich was waiting to receive and Perez and Buchman, the other two, were moving for position. A small group of onlookers were well back under the basketball hoop, but none of the four were playing for the audience. This was the finals of the Seniors Doubles Handball Championship of 1984, and collectively there was close to a quarter of a millennium of experience on the floor. Sid and Perez were up two to one, and had just won service at fourteen to ten. He lofted an incredibly accurate service that bounced an inch inside the back corner and positioned himself for the return. Reich hit a solid shot that Perez dinked back down the side. The alarm went off before Sid could replay Buchman's backhand and his own plunging lefthanded crosscourt put-away for the match. No matter, he'd rewind the reel and run it again some other night as he had for the past four years.

Sid shifted and put his feet over the side of the bed. His watch said 1:30. I'm too old to be doing this, he thought, and walked quietly to the window. After a minute he picked out the form of the dog lying prone on the dock. Sid waited several minutes, but the animal didn't move a muscle.

Sid had already figured out a route. Fortunately the fire escape was positioned along the back wall of the guest house and passed right next to his window. He stepped out on it and quietly started down. His crepe-soled shoes didn't make any noise at all, but the problem was dodging the flower pots and window boxes the other guests had placed beneath their own windows. The back lawn sloped down to the water so he was three flights up on the fire escape while only two from the front entranceway. He made it to the floor below and was halted by the cantilevered bottom ladder. Here was a more serious problem. If he started the ladder swinging down he didn't think he could control its momentum, and the metal weight was sure to bang noisily against the metal stop. He looked around for something to use as a cushion but the only things he saw were ceramic pots. He didn't want to risk another trip back up to his room so he bent down, removed one of his shoes, and laced it in place. Then he unlatched the bottom ladder and watched as it swung down. The resulting noise was muffled by the wedged crepe sole, but Sid still waited another minute before moving. No lights came on, so with one shoe off and one on, he stepped out onto the back lawn.

Sid walked quickly in the direction of the water. He gave a wide berth to the sleeping dog and stepped up onto the dock. Two more steps brought him to the side of the little boat. He turned around to make one more check, but the guest house was still quiet and dark under the cloudy sky. Then he knelt down and got into the boat.

He had been in one of these before, a long time ago when he and Emma had taken a day at Rye Playland. Basically they were two molded seats side by side, which went into a raised portion in the back covering the paddle wheel. A pair of bicycles on pontoons. This particular model had two vinyl cushions on the seats as an added comfort feature for the guests. Everything else was either the smooth surface of fiberglass or the chromed steel of the steering bar and drive pedals. Sid had brought a little flashlight with him and his eyes followed along in the little circle of light as it played across the boat. He didn't know what he was looking for, perhaps a little knob or lever . . . something out of the ordinary. In a couple of minutes he had given the top a onceover but had seen nothing unusual. He hung himself over the edge of the back cowling and shone his light underneath, but there was still nothing. The only thing left was the part of the boat under the water, but he wasn't about to go for a swim and it was too dark anyway. He tried stretching his arm underneath along the sides, but all he felt was a slimy undercarriage. There was still a big portion of the boat underneath that he hadn't been able to reach. He sat back in the seat and cursed softly. Maybe he was wrong and the boat had nothing to do with it. But it made no sense. Why the dog, why the route so close to the Trumpy? He looked in the seat next to him, the one Franco sat in, and frowned. Then it hit him, and he shook his head, annoyed at his own stupidity. He leaned over and carefully ripped the vinyl cushion from its Velcro stays. He

didn't need the flashlight to see the tiny trapdoor and re-
cessed release button. Once he popped the door open to
look inside, the mechanism he saw was as simple as it was
ingenious. A brass track ran down into the water and in it
was a sliding bar on a ratchet with a big hook at its lower
end and a release handle at the top. Sid noticed that the
hook had a safety device at its open end to keep something
locked in place once it was snagged. All Franco had to do
was lower the bar and the hook would protrude a good two
feet under the boat. Then at any time later he could lift it
back up and retrieve what he had caught. Sid carefully
lowered the door and heard it click in place. Then he re-
positioned the cushion and sat back. Now that he knew
what to look for, he noticed a little red dot on the front of
the boat that corresponded to the position of the hook. He
must use that as a guide to direct the boat over the underwater pickup point. Very clever, Sid thought, and quietly
got out of the boat. The water made little rippling sounds
as it slapped against its rocking side.

This time he passed a little closer to the sleeping dog
and made it to the fire escape without a sound. He climbed
back up to the weighted end of the ladder and paused to
take a breath. Suddenly a light somewhere up above him
went on and he flattened himself against the wall. A broad
trapezoid of yellow light fanned out on the back lawn, and
shortly thereafter, the shadow of someone's head. Sid
couldn't figure whose room it was coming from, but it was
definitely on the floor above, next to his. Was that Forstman's apartment, or Slater's, or worse yet, Franco's? He
didn't dare move. The shadow slipped away from the window but the light stayed on. Then, two, maybe three minutes later, the back lawn went dark. Sid breathed a little
deeper, but still waited. God, let's hope it was some old
insomniac, he thought, and finally took a step out toward

the end of the ladder. He left his shoe where it was for the moment, and reached up for the highest rung. Then he raised himself off the grill and hung there suspended. Slowly, very slowly, the end he was holding swung down. He rode it most of the way until its own momentum brought the long end of the ladder back up. He only let up when he heard the lock catch with what sounded to him like a shot. Again he hesitated, but this time there was no response. He undid his shoe, tiptoed up the last flight, and climbed in his window.

His adrenaline had been racing ever since he left his room, and now it took at least several minutes for his heart to stop pounding. He just lay on his bed and looked at the open window in wonder. "Christ," he said, "did I really do that?"

CHAPTER 32

...

"Thank the Lord it's Thursday," Mrs. Kass said and made a five letter word, *cruse* on the board around the U. She counted up the points and added them to her total.

"Aren't you forgetting something, dear?" Mrs. Epping said and looked sharply at her friend. "Like the I."

"If I had intended to spell *cruise* I would have spelled *cruise*," she sniffed. *Cruse* happens to be a small pot for holding water." She grinned. "Now, if you happen to be holding the q, which I think you are, you're stuck."

Mrs. Epping fumed and looked toward Sid. "Did you ever hear of such a thing? *Cruse*. I let her get away with murder." Sid shrugged and looked down at his own letters. Scrabble had never been his favorite game, but a good one, nonetheless, for kibitzing.

"What's so special about Thursday?" he asked and moved some letters around on his rack. P-C-R-D-E-F-J, J-E-R-D-F-P-C, F-R-E-D-P-J-C?? He finally settled for *red* and waited his turn.

"Thursday is when Doctor Grimes comes," Mrs. Kass said. "Ten o'clock he comes and visits all of us who have complaints. In our own room too, imagine."

"That's right," Mrs. Epping added. "He comes to check that all of us are healthy. Most of us came here because of him." She leaned forward and laid down the letters Q-U-I-T against Mrs. Kass's e. "You didn't think I had my own u," she said, gloating. "That's twenty-eight points, dear. Oh, I do love it when you turn such a lovely red."

128

Sid played his word. "That's nice of him. Do you all pay for his visits?"

"Indirectly," Mrs. Epping answered, reaching for more letters from the bag of tiles. "You'll soon notice your monthly bill going up. They started me at six hundred a month and now I'm way over a thousand. Whenever I complain it's Doctor Grimes's visits they always point to, and how can you argue with that?"

"You can't argue anyway," Mrs. Kass interjected. "It's in the D code . . . stage three."

"Fortunately, Mr. Epping saved enough before he left me," Mrs. Epping continued. "I don't need to worry about money until I'm ninety-five." She smiled. "But then most of the guests here are well off. And from what I can tell, most don't have any relatives either."

"That's right," Mrs. Kass added. "The idea is to drop dead a day before you run out of money. Unless, of course, you do it a moment after you lay down a seven-letter word on the triple word score using the q and the z. That'd be heaven."

"Looks like," Sid said absently, "the management here is doing everything they can to speed the process up."

"What?" they both asked at the same time.

"Nothing," Sid said, and leaned forward. "What's the score?"

"Don't even look," Mrs. Kass said lightly. "You're playing with a pair of pros."

■ ■ ■

Sid was waiting downstairs at ten o'clock when Doctor Grimes arrived. He'd never seen the man before, but it was obvious from the moment he set foot inside the hall who the gentleman was. Dark hair graying at the temples, expensive clothes, black bag, stethoscope. Very natty. He could have come from Central Casting for an appearance on "General Hospital." The only difference was he never would have passed the voice test. Dr. Grimes's was not the kind you'd want in a friendly physician. It was more suited to a croupier on the lobster shift at a Vegas casino, or someone who had smoked too many cigarettes.

"Morning," he said as he passed by on his way to the office. "You must be Rossman."

Sid nodded.

"Are you down for a checkup?"

"Not today. I didn't even know about it."

"Well, next time perhaps," the doctor said and moved away. "Good to meet you."

Sid leaned farther back in his chair. "Good to meet you too," he murmured and watched Grimes enter the office and close the door behind him. "I'm sure."

■ ■ ■

"I think we have a problem," William Forstman said to the other man. "Franco thinks the dog was drugged. He has a hard time standing up. Franco's never seen him like that."

Grimes's eyes narrowed. "You check? Anything missing downstairs?"

Forstman shook his head. "Maybe it's just something he ate."

"That's smart," the doctor said sarcastically. "Of course it's something he ate. How do you think they drug dogs. Check his stool. See if anything turns up." He shook his head. "The last thing we need is more complications. We got it down to a sweet operation now and I don't want anything to complicate things." He hesitated for a moment. "Someone from the inside?"

"I don't see some geriatric hero here," Forstman said.

"Curious, maybe, like Schecter, but nothing like drugging a dog."

Grimes made a face. "Who else then? On the outside it's all covered. Everyone's happy with their cut. We've worked with them before. . . . No, I don't see it. It's inside." He paced back and forth in the little office. "I don't believe this. It's not that you don't have enough leverage here, Willie. A twenty-million-a-year operation and you can't keep a bunch of old farts in line. You manipulate their drugs, alter their food, control their outside movements, seems to me they should be eating out of your hand. This should be the best front in town." He stopped to glare at the other man. "Goddamn it, get it right. If someone inside is playing detective, I want to know who it is, then I want to know what you're going to do about it. Is that understood?"

The man with the gold chains nodded.

"Good. Now, I suppose it's time I started up in the rooms. How many you got for me this week?"

"Here's the list. Eight of them are waiting."

"Just my luck, with a golf date at eleven. Willie, I mean it. This is not a game we're playing. It's deadly serious business. I make a good living as a doctor. I don't need all these complications."

"Even for twenty million a year?"

Grimes glowered at him. "Just take care of it."

■ ■ ■

Forty-five minutes later when Doctor Grimes left, Sid was still camped out on the chair in the hallway reading a copy of *Golf Digest*, a magazine as relevant to the guests in the hotel as *Motorcycle World*. He peered over the top of an article about using the wind to control your slice as the doctor made one last stop at the office, then walked past. This time he didn't even bother with a nod. Sid watched as he put his bag down, fumbled with its lock, then slammed the door behind him. He raised the magazine again and looked at the diagram of a controlled slice, but it wasn't getting through. What was, however, was the peculiar little detail Sid had just noticed. The black bag Grimes had arrived with had a chrome lock. The one he had just put down had a brass one. Everything else was the same. Now isn't that peculiar, Sid thought.

CHAPTER 33

...

Twenty-four hours after leaving the police station, Margaret was still having a hard time controlling her anger.

"Can you believe they threatened to lock me up?" she blurted out. Berdie and Durso looked up from the newspapers they were reading at the dinette. This was the fourth interruption since the breakfast dishes had been cleared away, so they were not unprepared.

"Well, you did throw a punch at one of the cops," Durso said with a grin. "I'm actually surprised they let you get off so easily."

Margaret reddened. "That was not a punch. I was merely making a point and got carried away."

"Very carried away," Berdie added, going back to the paper.

"Well, it wasn't right. They treated us like a bunch of criminals. Carl's boat got damaged trying to help and then they slap him with a big fine."

"He was happy to pay it," Durso answered. "Said it was worth the excitement."

"That's not the point." Margaret came and sat down next to them.

Berdie put the paper down with resignation. She could tell when her friend was just warming up.

"The point is, they didn't listen. They never listen. They're so wound up in their own little chains of command and protocol that they can't see the forest through the trees."

"I think that's for,'" Durso corrected. "For the trees. You always get that wrong."

Margaret waved it away. "Whatever. They're given a golden opportunity and they treat us like we're the culprits."

"But we're the ones that barreled down those canals like they were bowling alleys," Durso said. "They told us they got at least two dozen calls."

"I suppose those people that called would rather have their kids wind up in some detox program." Margaret shook her head. "It just makes me angry, and then they didn't even bother to call Diamond as I asked."

"What good would that have done?" Berdie asked.

"It would have made us look less foolish."

"I'm not so sure," Durso said and stood up. "Listen, Margaret. We're lucky no one was hurt, and we're lucky that the police treated it with a little good humor. It was when you started throwing punches . . ."

"They were not punches . . ."

". . . that things got sticky. I'm just glad we're out of it, that's all."

"Well, we're not," Margaret said. "Not yet. If we can't attack the problem from the water, we'll attack it from the land. Sid's still at Forstman's." She turned to Berdie. "I think it's time for some rehearsals."

"How's that?" Berdie asked but her eyes gave her away. She knew what was coming.

"Time for Sid's cousin to make her appearance."

"Oh God," she sighed. "I was afraid of that.

CHAPTER 34

...

Franco held up the empty garbage bag for Forstman to see. There was nothing unusual about it except for the fact that a big piece at one of its lower corners was gone. What appeared to be the missing piece lay on Forstman's desk on top of a brown bag.

"The smaller piece is from Shadow . . . about an hour ago. The plastic's the same color as the kind we use so I had the housekeeper check all the rooms. The bag came from the new guy's room . . . Rossman. There's no doubt he did it. Son of a bitch almost killed the dog."

Forstman looked carefully at the two exhibits without saying anything. After he had satisfied himself with Franco's analysis, he closed his eyes and began rubbing an imaginary spot on his temple.

"Rossman, huh?"

"Yeah. Now why'd he want to do a thing like that?"

"I don't know." He opened his eyes and fixed them on the larger man. "But I sure would like to find out. Think you could arrange that?"

Franco nodded and his lantern jaw dropped to accommodate the beginning of a smile.

"And Franco," Forstman added, "if Mr. Rossman is uncooperative, perhaps you could find a way to arrange for another vacancy here at the hotel. You understand?"

The smile kept coming. "I do," Franco said. "Perfectly. Mr. Rossman has already expressed an interest in a boat trip."

"That'll do nicely," Forstman said and looked once again at the ripped bag. "Very nicely."

■ ■ ■

From his seat near the window in one of the side rooms, Sid saw Berdie coming before anyone else did, but it didn't matter. The doors were still locked so he had to wait. She trundled up the sidewalk and turned into the entranceway, then disappeared as she mounted the front steps. She was all alone, but no matter, Sid still breathed a sigh of relief. Her appearance meant he could get word out to Margaret and shortly there'd be some real help, maybe Diamond or Moorehead. Just get me out, he thought, I've got all I need. He moved into the hallway, took a seat midway, and once again picked up *Golf Digest*. He got back to his familiar slice diagram as the doorbell rang. Good old Berdie, Sid thought. I'll never kid her about those pigeons again.

There was some muffled exchange on the front intercom, then, after a few moments, Forstman himself went and opened the door. He passed Sid without saying a word, but then, as though from thin air, Donna Slater appeared. She sat down in the chair next to Sid and looked silently his way. Sid felt extraordinarily uncomfortable but kept his nose buried in the magazine. He tried to hear what Forstman was saying to Berdie on the front stoop, but the noise of the television nearby masked their exchange. He'd just have to wait, and the hell with Slater's rudeness.

"I'm afraid you are mistaken," Forstman said. "We don't have anyone here by that name. No Rossmans, Russmans, or anything else that sounds like it. You must have the wrong guest house."

"But he called me the day he checked in," Berdie insisted. "The Forstman Guest House on North Bay Road. I wrote it down." She was trying not to get flustered, but this was one scenario that had not been rehearsed. She'd just have to wing it.

"Perhaps he decided to go elsewhere. In fact, now that I think about it, we did have an older gentleman inquire about a room earlier in the week, but when I mentioned our charges, he said he couldn't afford them and took off. Kind of a well-built gentleman with white hair. That him?"

Berdie nodded instinctively. "But he said he was staying," she stammered. "Absolutely."

"He changed his mind," Forstman said and this time there was a note of finality in the tone. "He is not with us. Now if you'll excuse me . . ."

"But I'm his only relative. How am I going to find him?" she said desperately. "He told me to visit him here."

"Oh no, that couldn't be," Forstman said. "We never allow unannounced visits from anyone, relatives or not. See, there must be some mistake." He opened the door just enough for him to pass back through and started closing it.

"His first name is Sid," Berdie called desperately. "You're sure?"

"We have no Sids here!" Forstman said and closed the door with some force.

■ ■ ■

Twenty feet away Sid flinched, perhaps because of the door slam, but most likely because of the last thing Forstman said, the only bit of conversation he clearly heard. He lowered the magazine slowly and looked directly at Donna Slater.

"No unannounced visits," she said simply.

CHAPTER 35

...

This was serious. Sid tried the door again but it was still locked. The door handle turned in his hand, but the heavy door didn't even rattle on its hinges. "Damn!" He kicked at it but only succeeded in bruising his toes. After escorting him to his room, Franco had said Donna Slater would bring him his dinner. That meant a full lockup until at least tomorrow. Whatever stage of the D code this was, it was serious . . . serious enough to start some honest-to-goodness worrying. What had they found? He walked to his bed and lay down. Berdie was sure to tell Margaret, but even with Moorehead or Diamond it might take them a day to spring him. By then . . . who knows? Franco had laid on a pedal boat ride for ten. He got up again and paced to the window. They hadn't overlooked anything. Two large nails had been driven home so that only a small crack, something under an inch, remained open. Without a tool it was impossible to remove them.

"For fresh air," Franco had said with a smugness that tried Sid's control. "And don't try breaking the window. We'd hear it and bill your account." He had laughed then and walked out, slamming the door shut with a loud and ominous click.

Sid looked through the window and saw the dog. It didn't matter if he could get onto the fire escape again. Shadow looked as if he was just waiting to return the favor of being drugged and nearly killed the night before. He had fully recovered and was now pacing back and forth along the dock with nervous energy. No, Franco hadn't needed the nails at all.

So then what, wait? Sid didn't like the odds, especially with Mr. Schecter as an indication of the house's vigorish. The only thing to do was to go on the offensive. If he was still around in the morning he'd go on the pedalboat outing with a little something up his sleeve. The more he thought about it, the more he liked the idea. He'd make his escape by water. Perfect . . . except for one minor detail: Franco.

In Sid's youth, all the young toughs on the block had blackjacks. Now it was all guns, from little .22s to big .357 Magnums. But back in the depression years of the thirties guns were only for the successful gangsters; the kids practiced mayhem with homespun ingenuity. Brass knuckles, belt buckles, straight-edge razors, car antenna zip guns, and of course, the sap. If used skillfully it could knock down a man in one blow, or kill him in a few more. Its history was long and widespread, and with good reason. Saps were wonderfully concealable and easy to make.

Sid opened his drawer and got out his longest pair of socks. They were a nice, strong cotton weave and reached up to his calves. Sand would have been best, or a heavy piece of metal, but Sid didn't have the luxury of those items. He scanned the room for some substitute and his eyes came to rest on a little flat ceramic ashtray. On the side of it was the name of some restaurant in Hallandale. It was about three inches square and a half inch high with a depression in the middle. It was too wide as is, but broken in half it would do just fine. Sid took a pencil and placed it crosswise in the grooves made for cigarettes. Then he turned it upside down, held one side down with a foot, and stamped down on the other side. The ashtray cracked right in half over the pencil. Carefully, Sid wrapped the halves back to back with a strip of paper, slid them down to the toe of one sock, folded the sock over, then slid that down into the toe of the other one. He put a knot at the base of the bulge, and one at the open end of the sock. When he was finished he picked it up and felt its weight. A quarter of a pound easy. Then he swung it down onto his pillow in a quick overhand arc and smiled at the noise and deep depression it made. Perfect, more so because it slid right down the sleeve of his jacket with nothing showing. The knot at the bottom of the sock was only a half inch inside his sleeve and ready at a moment's notice. Now, he thought, the odds are a little more even.

But Sid had no illusions about his chances one to one against Franco. His only trump card was surprise, and if that failed, it would be nice to have a little help. But how the hell to get the police there. The door was locked, the window was closed. He sat down heavily on the bed and looked again. Well, not closed entirely . . . but what good was an inch?

The making of the blackjack had brought him back fifty-five years, to George Washington High School up on Audubon Avenue. His next jump brought him back even farther, to grammar school, P.S. 2 on Henry Street on the Lower East Side. Slowly, he got up, took a step over to the window, and put his eyes down to the narrow opening. Through it he could see the railings of the fire escape, then open space. He stood up and looked into that openness, and slowly the idea began to take shape. Approximately twenty feet beyond the side of the building, the width of the driveway and strip of bushes, was the fence of the next property. On the other side Sid could see the beginnings of a lawn, then a line of what looked like fruit trees. If there was a house it was somewhere back by the water behind the trees and out of his vision. The fence was maybe eight feet high, but Sid still had two stories on it. If he could get a good snap, it might carry. As well as he could remember, he took inventory of everything he needed: paper, pen, tape, wire, elastic, stick. The first two items were easy. Forstman's was not classy enough to have its own stationery in the desk drawer, but Sid found something better, the heavy, blue blotter on top. Sid wrote the message on it with his fountain pen, then began folding it. He had no tape, so he used the half-dozen bandaids he always traveled with. He thought about using coat hanger wire, but then decided on his umbrella instead. What the hell, he could buy a new one for three bucks in any shoe store in town. Dismembering it, he removed two lightweight pieces of aluminum and bent them into shape. For the stick he used the umbrella shaft, then looked around for the most important element, the elastic.

But of course he didn't have any. He looked everywhere in the room, but there wasn't a rubber band, or for that matter, an elasticized waistband to be had. How could you make a paper airplane with struts and all and catapult it out into space without elastic. He looked again, this time taking the bed apart in the hope that the mattress pad was held in place with elastic, or even that there were fitted sheets, but no luck. Nothing. He sat down on the floor and looked painfully at his wonderful paper plane. In grade school they used to fly these things sometimes over ninety feet. It was all in the way you bent the paper, and after sixty years, Sid still remembered. Its wing span was at least sixteen inches, held rigid by the taped umbrella strut, and from its nose protruded the second belly strut, bent into a hook to accept the elastic. It was three inches high, but the fuselage would bend under the wing to clear the window. Perfect, but grounded without elastic. What did they use at P.S. 2, cut inner tubes? Fat chance of him finding one in his closet. Damn, even his socks were ribbed. He looked down at them but his mind was still thinking about the long black rubber strips. It was the color that finally made the association, and he sat up with a jerk. Emma, bless her neat compulsive soul, had always said never travel without them, and by God, he never had, although what he needed a pair of black rubber Totes for in Florida was anybody's guess. He rummaged for them now in the bottom of his suitcase and found them wedged into a corner next to the fancy wingtips he had brought for special occasions. All he needed was a sharp knife, or better yet, his razor.

It took him only half an hour, and in the end he had what he wanted. The Totes looked as if they'd been caught in a lawn mower, slivers of black rubber lay around him like so many scraps in an egg noodle factory, but he had sliced out two long thick strips. Knotted together, then into a single loop, they became a homemade rubber band fifteen inches long. When stretched, it doubled in length and had enough snap when released to break a china cup.

He brought the plane over to the desk and wrote on both of the wings, "Read me, important message inside," then fitted the rubber band to the nose hook. The other end of the elastic he tied very tightly to the end of the umbrella shaft with a piece of string. Like a little kid with his first model airplane, he made a few short test flights inside the room, then took everything over to the window. Now came the tricky part, piloting it over both the fire escape railing in front of the window and then over the fence onto the neighboring lawn. He was convinced that if the damn thing made it, someone would pick up the strange-looking blue object. If it didn't . . .

He carefully bent the fuselage under the wing, then pushed the plane through the half-inch opening. Once it was through, he bent the fuselage back down with his fingertips. Now the umbrella shaft, point first. Halfway out the elastic began to stretch and he had to hold tightly to the tail of the plane. He pushed the umbrella farther until he reached the curved handle. If he let it go, the plane would have flown beautifully the three feet into the fire escape railing and have been torn to pieces. But by rotating the curved umbrella handle inside the window, he was able to raise the point just enough to clear the top metal railing. Or so he hoped, because he couldn't hold onto the plane any longer. It slipped from his straining fingertips and shot outward. The bottom of the fuselage hit the rail and the plane jumped another two inches higher. The ricochet jammed the fuselage up toward the wing and instead of flying straight, the plane started angling slightly to the right. While it was now headed more directly over the fence, it was also on a collision course with a tall pine tree on the edge of Forstman's back driveway. Sid watched in horror as the blue piece of paper, as large as a New York pigeon with wings outstretched, glided slowly on the warm afternoon breeze. It was still ten feet away from the tree, still curving. Sid was sure it was going to hit it and get stuck, or worse yet, bounce back. Then, at the last second, he saw the needles of the tree bend to a little puff of wind, the same puff that nudged Sid's plane a few inches to the right and past the edge of the pine. Sid continued watching as the plane flew on, clearing the top of the stockade fence by a good five feet. He followed it down until it curved past the edge of his building and he could no longer see it. He let out the chestful of air he had been holding and steadied himself on the window frame. Little Stinky Rossman never had a better plane, he thought with a grin, even when the pot was for two hundred baseball cards. He cleaned up the rubber strips on the floor, rewrapped the umbrella with the black band inside, then went back to his bed. The fact that he couldn't go down to dinner didn't bother him. On a bet, he wasn't going to let anything from Forstman's kitchen inside his stomach again.

CHAPTER 36

...

The phone rang in Doctor Grimes's office while he was explaining to one of his patients what was meant by a double bypass. He had an earnest expression on his face, but it changed immediately when he heard the voice on the other end. Forstman spoke in a hurry and didn't even bother apologizing for the indiscretion of calling during examining hours. What he had to say was too important.

"We found the son of a bitch. It was the last guy you sent."

"Excuse me?" Grimes said and turned to one side.

"The guy that drugged the dog, Rossman. He's only been here a few days. Don't tell me that's a coincidence. Someone sent him."

The doctor took a glance at his patient, who looked lost in a fog of despair.

"You sure?"

"Positive. The piece of plastic around the food the dog ate came from his room. Then Slater told me she gave him some pills that afternoon. What more you want?"

"Your plans?"

"Don't worry about that. Franco's arranging something. But how'd you get him? That's what I'm wondering."

"A recommendation. One of my patients, some elderly lady claimed she had chest pains."

"A new patient?"

Grimes was silent for a minute. Finally he answered, "Yes."

"What'd she look like?"

He tried to remember, then gave a brief description of Margaret.

"Do yourself a favor," Forstman continued. "Last week the *Herald* had a story about a bunch of old people running some kind of sightseeing service for old people in guest houses. She came to see us with the clipping. I kicked her out, but I think that's when Schecter got his note out. There's a picture with the story. See if it's her. Maybe Rossman's in it too."

Grimes only grunted and his patient looked up, thinking the doctor himself was having chest pains.

"If it is," Forstman continued, "there may be an address or number where they can be found."

"Okay," Grimes said, and turned back to his patient with a smile. "I'll take care of it . . . professionally." He hung up softly.

"A problem?" the man sitting in front of him asked.

Grimes stared at him blankly, then finally shook his head.

"It's another patient." He picked up the X rays on his desk and tapped them lightly. "Consider yourself lucky, Mr. Gold, you're only facing a double bypass."

CHAPTER 37

...

At nine forty-five Sid heard the lock on the door release and then a moment later, Franco's knock. That's polite, Sid thought sarcastically, as if I have a choice. He opened the door to see Franco standing there, blocking eighty percent of the opening.

"Good morning, Mr. Rossman," he said easily. "Ready for our little boat ride?" He looked over Sid's shoulder at the table with the untouched breakfast dishes. "What's the matter, not feeling hungry?"

"Indigestion," Sid said simply. "Yeah, let's go." He passed by Franco and headed for the staircase. He was ready. He'd been ready since seven o'clock when he woke up. The blackjack was nestled up the inside of his left sleeve with the knot just hidden inside his cuff. And the twenty hours without food hadn't affected him at all. At least it didn't seem to. The adrenaline pumping through his bloodstream masked any feelings of hunger or fatigue. He kept telling himself it would all be over soon, maybe a half hour, maybe less. He just had to be patient, wait his opportunity, strike when the other man wasn't looking.

Franco walked right next to him and directed him to a door that lead out to the side driveway. He closed the door behind them and motioned in the direction of the water. As Sid turned, he saw something that stopped him dead. The stockade fence on the other side of the driveway was the open variety with spaces between the boards. Unconsciously he had looked in the direction his plane had been taking, and there, maybe twenty feet on the other side he

146

saw it. Even though the shape was interrupted by the boards of the fence, the color was unmistakable. It had made a graceful landing next to a flowering azalea bush, and there it had remained, untouched and obviously unread.

"Come on, let's go," Franco raised his voice. "What's so interesting about the fence?"

"Nothing," Sid said and followed him. Except now the blackjack up his sleeve seemed to have lost all its heft. It felt more like two blocks of balsa wood than heavy ceramic.

"You take the right side," Franco commanded when they were on the little dock.

Sid climbed aboard and slid into the seat. There was still a little dampness on it from the evening's mist, but what made him really uncomfortable was the chill. The temperature on the water must have been ten degrees lower than by the hotel, and Sid was only wearing a light sports jacket. His feet found the pedals in front of him. Maybe the exercise would keep him warm.

Franco cast off, levered his big frame into the left-hand seat, and started pedaling slowly. In a few seconds they were well away from the shore. Franco was steering and made a slow turn to the right, the same way he always went.

"Restful, ain't it?" Franco said.

Sid, about to jump out of his skin from anxiety, simply nodded.

"You know what's amazing, Mr. Rossman, this canal looks like a little stream, right? Take a guess at how deep it is."

"I don't know," Sid leaned over the edge to take a look. "Five, eight feet?"

"Looks that way, don't it. You'd never guess there was more than twenty feet of water under us, would you?"

Sid didn't bother shaking his head. He got the impression it wasn't really a question, more like a lead-in. It turned out he didn't have long to wait for the follow-up.

"Sometimes when the tide's running, there's a pretty swift current runs through here, enough to give even strong swimmers a problem. Deceptive with all these channels."

"Is it?" Sid asked. "I suppose it's not a very good idea then to go swimming." He gave his pedals a little extra shove but it was damped by Franco's steady motion. There was a slight current running against them, but the boat was still making headway up the canal. They hadn't moved out of the center yet toward the Trumpy, but it was still a good 200 yards away. Sid wouldn't even consider using the sap until after they passed her . . . unless he had to.

"Tell me, Franco," Sid said, changing the subject. "You been with Mr. Forstman long?"

Franco laughed and leaned back in his seat. "Mr. Rossman, I think you got it all wrong." He looked over at him and a light came into his eyes that could have pierced inch-thick armor plate. "It's gonna be my job to ask the questions. It's gonna be your job to stay dry."

CHAPTER 38

...

Margaret had the motor on and transmission in gear when she saw the little man running down the steps of the Glenmore Rest House. She was about to pull out and drive to the police station as Berdie had insisted over breakfast, but there was something in the man's agitated haste . . . she kept her foot on the brakes and waited to see which way he turned. Maybe it was a sixth sense, but she wasn't surprised when he came directly toward them. As he got nearer she saw it was the manager. She lowered the window as he came over.

"I just got a call," he said, slightly out of breath. "Some place up on Bay Road. They got an urgent message for you. Some crazy story . . . something about a paper airplane." He took a piece of paper from a pocket and unfolded it. "I got it here, word for word." He passed it through the window. "Said they just found it."

"Thank you," Margaret said and began reading at the top. Before she was halfway through there were frown lines at the corners of her eyes. When she finished, she took a quick look at her watch.

"Good Lord," she whispered. "There's no time."

"For what?" Durso asked from the dinette behind her.

"To keep Sid from winding up on an obituary page. It's after ten. He's probably already on the water." She took a quick look around her at the large Winnebago, then looked out the front window toward Collins Avenue. Without hesitating she pulled the key out of the ignition and opened her door. "Come on, we have to hurry. We'll leave the van and

149

take a cab. I have no idea how to get there from land and even if I did, we might not be able to park this big thing. It's our only hope."

"Where are we going?" Durso asked, putting on a windbreaker and following her out.

"Carl's boat is being repaired," she answered. "The only place left is Pete Feezel's."

Berdie groaned, but Margaret didn't hear it. By that time she was ten yards ahead of them and whistling for a taxi.

■ ■ ■

Feezel was out back when they arrived. He was in his shirtsleeves trying to convince a prospective boat buyer that the twenty-three-foot Wellcraft in front of them could handle the ocean easy.

"You don't need anything bigger," he was saying with conviction. "Throw a two hundred Merc on her and she'll do the Bahama Bank and back in a day." He looked up and stopped talking when he saw the three old people hurrying his way. At first he didn't recognize them, but as they came closer he nodded.

"Carl's friends, right?"

"Yes," Margaret said. "Have you got a minute?"

"Yeah, hold on." He turned to the buyer and told him to climb aboard the Wellcraft. "Here's the ladder," he said. "You look around for as long as you like. The cabin is unlocked. Let me know what you think." He held the ladder for him, then turned back to Margaret.

"So, you ever find that Trumpy?"

"We did, thanks. Now we need some more help."

"Shoot."

"We need to rent one of your boats, one of those ski boats I saw last time." She tried her best to keep the urgency out of her voice. "We won't need it long, maybe a half hour."

Feezel looked at the three of them skeptically. "You know how to drive one of them?"

"Carl showed me," Margaret said without hesitation. "There won't be a problem. We just want to do some sight-seeing around Sunset Isles, so we won't be going fast." She started fidgeting with her handbag, trying to open it. "Whatever it costs we'd pay . . ."

"Hell, take her for half an hour, take her for an hour. You don't need to pay. I got three of those boats and not one of them is out today in this miserable weather. Carl's bought enough of my boats for me to give his friends a hand." He motioned for them to follow. "They're all ready to go for skiing, but I don't think that'll matter. Here, take number three. She's got the best motor." He fumbled on a board of keys until he found the one for number three, then dropped down into the cockpit. The boat was not nearly as large as Carl's, but it was no rowboat either. It had a 125 Evinrude that made a throaty rumbling as Feezel kicked it over. There was a driver's seat and a seat next to it for the spotters. The rest of the boat was open.

"Here's the controls," Feezel said. "Just take it easy at first until you get the feel of it. Toward you for reverse, up for forward. There's plenty of gas, you could make it up to Golden Beach and back if you wanted." He reached up for Margaret's hand. "Come on, that's right, hop down. In case you want them, you'll find the life belts in the storage compartment over there." He waited until all three of them were seated comfortably, then swung himself up on the dock and untied the mooring lines. "Remember, slow at first. You'll get the hang of it in no time. Before you know it you'll be back to buy one."

Margaret smiled, then leaned forward so that her friends would hear.

"Life belts please," she said. "Just to be on the safe side."

"We're way ahead of you," Durso said, buttoning his up. After he was finished his hand found the side rail and he gripped it with determination.

"Ready" he said.

"Okay, here goes. I just hope we're not too late." She backed out of the slip, then turned ever so slowly until she was facing the open water. Feezel was already back with his client when he heard the high-pitched scream of the Evinrude and saw the three-foot roostertail leaping up behind the boat. By that time there was nothing he could do except pray that his insurance premiums wouldn't be affected.

CHAPTER 39

...

They were still moving steadily through the water, even though it seemed that Franco had slowed his pace. For his part, Sid kept his feet rotating on the pedals to keep warm, but there was no way he had any control over the motion of the boat. They were in the center of the canal, maybe 150 yards away from the Trumpy, but there was still plenty of time for Franco to turn toward the bigger boat, just in case there was a pickup scheduled.

"You know, Mr. Rossman," Franco said lazily, "Mr. Forstman is very fond of his possessions. All his possessions, including his dog."

"Looks like a nice animal," Sid offered, but he felt the involuntary tightening of a muscle in his back. The second time it twitched, Sid had to lean back hard on it to make it release.

"Was a nice animal," Franco added, "until someone drugged it. Now it's no good as a guard dog."

"Drugged? Who would do a thing like that."

"I thought you might have some idea," the big man said calmly.

Sid thought he was covered. They couldn't know. "Why, because my room is on the back and overlooks the dock?" he said.

"Not really. Lot of people overlook the dock." Franco reached into a pocket and withdrew a pack of cigarettes. He lit one up and flipped the match into the water. "Because yours was the only garbage bag missing a corner." He let that sink in for a minute. "Not missing really, we

153

found the little bag after it passed clean through the dog."
Franco sat up straight and stopped pedaling. "So you see,
there's no doubt who did it. Forstman wanted me to find
out why."

Sid remained silent for a moment. He watched as the
boat slowed in the soft current, then came to a stop. They
were the only ones out on the little canal and the silence
was a little eerie. Sid brought his left arm a little closer but
he didn't think he had a chance. Franco was looking right
at him. Maybe he could still bluff his way out.

"I don't like German shepherds," Sid said. "And I
didn't like the idea of being cooped up in the hotel because
some stupid dog needed a place to run. I thought the pills
would just get him sick." He shrugged. "Then he'd go
away."

Franco shook his head. "Not good enough, Mr.
Rossman. Not nearly good enough. You ever see *The God-
father,* the movie with Pacino and Brando?"

Sid frowned. "Yeah?"

"The scene where the brother is knocked off while he's
fishing in the little boat. Real easy-like. Bang. They tie
something heavy to his feet and leave the rest for the fishes.
It's twenty feet, Mr. Rossman, twenty feet." Franco took a
deep puff. "You can do better. Try again."

Sid was really sweating now. It ran down his back and
he felt it collect where his undershirt met his belt. Maybe
fifty degrees out and I'm sweating like the third game of a
singles match, he thought. But then he told himself he had
every reason to sweat. There was this bucket in the well
under Franco's legs, a bucket and a length of rope. Now for
the first time he noticed that the bucket wouldn't have been
any good for bailing. It was filled to the top with something
hard and pebbly, something like concrete. This wasn't turning out as he had planned . . . not at all.

He looked around again but he knew it was impossible. There were no police boats hiding around corners, no undercover cops lurking in private boats. His message had never been read. There were only the two of them, and the only thing that stood between him and a very wet death was maybe the truth, although that was doubtful, and one clumsy, homemade blackjack. Maybe, if he tried the first thing, he'd get a chance to use the second.

"It all started with Schecter," Sid began. "And the little note he passed. You know about the note?"

Franco nodded.

"So, all the rest was Margaret's idea; finding out about the boat, sending me in to investigate . . . I guess I didn't do too good a job. Anyway, it was all quite innocent. I drugged the dog, looked around, found nothing, and went back to bed. So you see, you got nothing to fear from me or my friends. Just a bunch of old-timers having a good adventure."

"I think you're lying," Franco said and began pedaling slowly. "I think you know enough to be a real problem." He stretched out his arm and put it innocently behind Sid's shoulder.

"Hey, wait a minute," Sid said nervously. "This is all a joke, right. You're just doing this to scare me."

"Oh no, Mr. Rossman. Mr. Forstman is a very serious man."

Sid brought his hands together and casually reached for the knot. He'd have to do something soon.

"But as long as I'm here, I got a little errand to do first." Franco said. "We're so close anyway. Besides, I thought you'd like to see how it all works. Hey, what's the point of killing you if you never knew the details." He chuckled maliciously and turned the tiller to the right. The little boat swung around until it was pointed directly at the

Trumpy. "Shipment comes in approximately once every two weeks. If something's waiting, there's a green bathing suit in the back window of the boat. I check every day. Simple, huh?" He gave the pedals a harder push. "We'll be there in two or three minutes. If you're a religious man, that should give you plenty of time."

Franco continued pumping away with his legs and the boat picked up speed. His arm was still around Sid, in case he had any ideas of escaping. Not that a swim would have helped. Franco could have been on top of him in the boat before he got five yards away. They traveled in silence for a minute. Even the splashing of the back paddle wheel seemed strangely remote to Sid.

"Did you kill Schecter too?" Sid finally asked.

"No, Mr. Schecter died of a heart attack. Everyone knows that. Just like they'll know you had a stroke and fell overboard while you were pedaling this boat." He smiled and pointed ahead of them. "There's *The Eternal Holidaze,* but I guess you already know about her." Franco shifted the tiller just slightly so they began to coast in parallel to her port side. The little pedal boat was about twelve feet out and still about twenty yards behind. It didn't take twenty-twenty vision to see the green bathing suit in the stern. Franco, once he noticed it, seemed to be intent on the water in front of them, and Sid followed his gaze. He almost didn't spot it until they were on top of it. Anyone who wasn't deliberately looking would have taken the wine cork as just another piece of flotsam from the waters around Sunset Isles. Franco steered so the cork passed right under the spot on the bow and a moment later Sid just barely felt the little tug beneath him. It was like the rudder getting caught on a fish line for a second before snapping it. The boat moved ahead as though nothing had happened and was past *The Eternal Holidaze* in another two yards.

"And that's all there is to it," Franco said. "Four kilos of coke. Nice way to go fishing, ain't it."

"Which you guys make into crack in the basement," Sid added.

"Oh, so the little man isn't so innocent," Franco said, and bent ever so slightly. Sid saw him reaching for the rope at his feet.

Now or never, he thought and pulled out the sap. He swung it over his head in an arc and brought it down with all his strength in the direction of Franco's right ear. But his windmill motion must have warned the other man; Franco flinched a few inches to the left. The weapon came crashing down on the side of his neck and ricocheted onto his shoulder. He let out a yelp, but yelps were not what Sid was hoping for. An inch to the left and he would have had silence.

Franco's hand grasped his neck, but his other hand, through some trained reflex, grabbed his attacker. Sid raised the sap for a second blow, but the big man buried his head into Sid's chest and his advantage was gone. The sap came down on Franco's broad back with a thump and simply bounced back up. Franco's only response to the blow was to tighten his grasp on Sid's shoulder. Then in one fluid motion, he took his hand away from his bruised and now bleeding neck and crashed it backhanded into the side of Sid's face. It was more of a slap than a punch, but it had enough force behind it to loosen two of Sid's teeth, split his cheek open, whip his head ninety degrees to the right, and knock him unconscious. The blackjack slipped from his limp hand and fell to the floor with a bump.

"Son of a bitch," Franco cursed and put his hand back

on his neck. With his other one he brought Sid back fully into the boat. He wasn't ready with the cement yet and they were still in a very exposed part of the canal. Franco knew a better place. A leisurely two-minute pedal would bring him around the next bend in the waterway, where there were only two houses, both of them set way back behind a screen of trees. That's where the son of a bitch will have his stroke and disappear forever, Franco thought. In private.

The pain in his shoulder was getting worse. A break maybe . . . clavicle or something. But it wouldn't keep him from tying a knot around Sid's legs and giving him a nudge over the side, followed by the bucket of concrete. Then it was only ten minutes back to the hotel. Franco looked at his victim. He was sitting upright with his head lolling to starboard, the blood making a little curve as it ran over his jaw and down under his collar. He had been planning a karate chop to the Adam's apple, which would have been much neater. Now he'd have to deal with the spattering of blood on the plastic deck of the pedalboat. Hell, there was water all around him. Wash it down in no time. He leaned Sid a little more inward, then bent down and started working on the rope. In half a minute he had the knot securely around Sid's ankles, and the bucket up on the sloping front deck. He let it slide until it was only a few inches from the edge, then held the rope tight. He took up the motion again with his feet and brought the boat into the beginning of the turn. Franco took a look behind him, but there was no one on the shore. No telling if anyone was looking from inside one of the houses, but even if they were they would probably figure them as two fishermen with a bucket of bait. He turned back, gave the pedals another few dozen rotations, and steered into the middle of the canal. It was still empty, although the opening to Biscayne Bay was no more than a hundred yards away.

"This is it, pops," he said and started pushing Sid toward the edge of the boat. Sid first went upright, then he leaned to starboard. One more push, Franco figured, and he'd be history, except at that moment a tiny fourteen-foot runabout puttered past the mouth of the canal. In it were a couple of teenagers, as far as Franco could figure out, maybe just out for a morning's hookey. They weren't looking his way, but he figured he'd play it safe. What's another minute, he thought.

A few seconds before the runabout cleared the mouth of the canal, Franco heard another noise, this coming up from behind him. He turned just in time to see a speedboat sweep around the curve with an old lady at the controls. She was thirty yards away and headed straight for him. Without thinking, he slammed the tiller over and started pedaling furiously. With the sudden movement, Sid's body slumped farther toward the water and stopped only when it hit the edge. His upper torso was tilted overboard and needed only a little nudge to flip him into the canal. Franco took his attention away from Sid and concentrated on avoiding the collision. He was only partially successful. The bigger boat just caught them in the port stern quarter and spun them two feet to the left. It was the same two feet that Sid bounced back into the boat. The collision tore the rope from Franco's grasp and sent the bucket of concrete overboard, still tied to Sid's legs. The rope tightened and pulled Sid back snugly to the edge, but the side was a little too high for it to pull him over. Instead, the bucket stayed just under the surface and acted as a sea anchor to slow the boat down. Franco cursed and pedaled harder, now pointing back the way he had come. The speedboat, he noticed, hadn't bothered to stop but was now doing a 180-degree turn at full throttle. In the confines of the canal, either the woman behind the wheel was an expert driver or crazy as hell.

■ ■ ■

Margaret's one clear thought on the six-minute bumpy ride over from Feezel's was just to get to the canals in time. She hadn't even bothered slowing for the occasional wake from passing boats. Her full attention was on finding the small southernmost opening in the first canal. She was hoping that once they got inside they'd find the pedalboat with the two men near the hotel. Then she'd pull alongside and improvise something.

But the last thing she expected to see was an empty canal. Between Forstman's and *The Eternal Holidaze* there wasn't so much as a rubber dinghy out. Nothing, and that made her really panic. She wove in and out of the first three canals a little slower than she had seen Carl do it, but there was still no one out on the water. Then she skidded around the last turn and suddenly saw them right in front of her. Her first reaction was to cut her speed, but her hand missed the throttle and the only thing left was to spin the wheel. The bow swung to the right and missed by inches. But boats don't turn like cars. Their pivot points are closer to the front, and Durso yelled, "Watch out!" just as the Bayliner clipped the smaller pedalboat. The glancing blow sent them into an even sharper turn. Margaret wrestled with the wheel and finally managed to straighten the boat out. She took a quick glance behind her, but she hadn't really needed a second look. Still vivid in her mind was the slumped and bloody form of Sid on the right-hand seat. It was enough to shatter any notion of improvisation. This was not the time for clever strategy. Even as she slammed the wheel all the way over and shouted to her two friends to hang on tight, all she knew was to get back to Sid and somehow get him on board.

Before turning the wheel, she hadn't seen the little dock jutting out into the canal, and she really didn't see it until the boat was halfway through the turn and committed to going the rest of the way. The dock loomed up almost out of nowhere and appeared to wait, perversely, while the boat continued to swing around on its unchangeable arc directly into a collision. For a split second, Durso actually thought of diving overboard, but the centrifugal force kept him stuck inside the boat like a kid in a roller coaster. Berdie closed her eyes and Margaret put her hands up, as if that would help in the high-speed impact. The bow kept swinging and by some miracle missed the end of the dock by no more than six inches. The stern cleared by half of that. In another second they were pointed back into the center of the canal and headed straight for the little pedalboat.

"Jesus Christ, that was close!" Durso shouted, all the color drained out of his face.

The first thing they had to do was stop Franco from getting closer to the guest house. Margaret swung up past him, then turned to block his path. As she did so, he turned underneath her and tacked off at an angle. She tried to get into reverse but it took her a few seconds to find it. By that time, he was past and she had to circle him again. This time she managed to keep her boat in front of him.

She hadn't even thought about a gun. Franco was wearing his attendant whites, so the sudden appearance of the little black revolver seemed entirely out of place. The tiny popping sound it made seemed harmless enough until Margaret noticed the result. The bullet shattered the windscreen a foot from Margaret's forehead. She didn't wait for a second bullet to test their luck, but hit the throttle and lurched ahead forty yards. It was apparently out of his range because he put the gun down on the seat next to him and began pedaling again. Margaret turned the boat to face him, then waited. She was still between him and the guest house some three blocks away, but now he was coming on boldly. When he got to within ten yards and picked up the revolver again, she threw it into reverse and kept her distance. He tried one shot just for the hell of it, but whatever weapon he was using, it was as accurate as a peashooter over that distance. The bullet stung the water five feet in front of them and skipped harmlessly away. Franco smiled for the first time since he had seen them, and put the gun back out of sight. The two boats, now moving in tandem and about twenty yards distance, were locked in some crazy Mexican standoff. It was a standoff that could continue for another several minutes until they reached the guest house. It was clear she had to do something before that. Sid was still alive, she could see him move now and then. How long that would last once they got him back into Forstman's was not something she cared to think about.

The only way was to use their speed. It was risky, but she had no choice. She backed up quickly, gaining about fifty yards on the other boat, then shifted into forward and slammed down the throttle.

"Get down!" she shouted. "On the floor where he can't see you."

"Good lord!" Berdie gasped but hit the wooden panels at her feet and clung on tight. Margaret put her face behind the steering wheel with her eyes just above the level of the front deck. She came in straight with the motor screaming and only veered off at the last second. The bullet came pretty close, blasting a hole in the fiberglass two feet away from Margaret's shoulder. The next one was off somewhere in the air as the little pedalboat rocked violently in the surge of water from the Bayliner's wake. This time Margaret slowed considerably before making the turn, then without hesitation came back at them from the rear.

The little boat was still rocking when they flew past again, this time on the other side. Once more Franco tried with the gun, but it was clear he was more intent on pedaling than on shooting. The bullet glanced off the cowling of the motor with a whine and made Berdie cross herself twice. Durso ventured a peek over the side when they were past and saw the little boat rocking so violently that Sid was now partially out of the boat.

"No more," he yelled at Margaret. "You'll send Sid overboard."

"We can't stop now," Margaret shouted.

This time she came in at a ninety-degree angle, setting up a wake that hit the bow of the little boat rather than the side. The gun popped again, but in the excitement they didn't hear it. They saw its effect, however, on the upholstery of the passenger seat. The bullet entered from the rear and tore out a great chunk of foam rubber from the front, right where someone's backbone would have rested. They watched breathlessly as the little boat bobbed over the waves they'd set up and Sid leaned a little closer to the water.

"Okay," Margaret said tightly, "That does it." She made another little circle and came in slowly to about five feet from the other boat. Franco stood up, braced himself, and aimed directly at her. The look on his face when the gun clicked on an empty chamber was priceless. Margaret let out her breath.

"I thought I counted six. Now, it's my turn." She pushed down on the throttle and the bigger boat slammed into the front of the pedalboat, sending Franco forward against the front panel. He just managed to keep himself from going over by grabbing the steering bar with both hands. In the process, the revolver bounced once on the front deck, then splashed into the water.

"Oh, no!" Durso screamed. The collision had jolted Sid a little bit farther out and he was now slipping over the edge. For a second he remained jackknifed over the gunwale, his head washing in the water and his legs slipping up the side to follow. Then, at the last moment before tumbling in, his hand reached out and found the grab rail. He pulled his head out of the water, gasped for breath, and struggled to get his body into the boat. For a second Margaret looked on in panic at his struggle, then she backed up, swung the boat in a quarter circle, and rammed in on the side Franco was sitting on. Sid tumbled back into his seat, Franco was thrown out against their bow keel, and the pedalboat splintered where it had been hit.

"Keep on the gas," Durso said. "Move him back into the middle. He's trying to get to the side."

After losing his gun, Franco had realized he couldn't make it back to the guest house and was now angling off to one of the banks. He was pedaling furiously trying to get away. The little boat broke free of the Bayliner and started splashing for the side. Sid sank down lower in his seat and continued to gulp in air.

"He's getting away," Berdie shouted. She had ventured a look after Durso showed that it was safe, and now was involved in the action. "Cut him off."

But Margaret already had the boat moving forward and before Franco could get fifteen feet away, the bigger boat shot in front of him. Margaret nosed her bow back into his side and continued to push him into the center of the canal. This time Franco reversed his motion, and after a minute, the little boat broke away again, this time in reverse. The sweat was pouring off his brow as he pumped and steered now for the other bank, but to no avail. Margaret caught him and, like a seal with a ball, she toyed him back where he had come from . . . and then some. Franco finally looked around and saw that it was hopeless. In the last few minutes his little boat had been pushed past where the drama had begun. It was clear that if this kept up the old lady could force him straight out of the canal into Biscayne Bay and attract the attention of a passing boat. As he saw it, he only had one option left. He waited until the right moment, then made a lunge from his seat to get on board the other boat.

He was almost quick enough. He managed to grab a little flag stanchion and begin to pull himself on board as best he could with his bruised shoulder. But Margaret had been waiting for it. She flipped the gear lever and hit the throttle and the Bayliner shot backward. Franco dangled for a moment with his legs making a parallel set of wakes behind him, then dropped off into the frothy water. He came up right away, cursed once, then began swimming for the little pedalboat, now some twenty yards away.

There was no way Margaret could stop him. She tried once, but he merely dove beneath their boat and kept going underwater. He took one deep breath next to the splintered pedalboat, then went under it. When he came up a moment later, she saw he was struggling with a water-proof parcel. Then he dove under again and headed for the nearest bank. She watched the trail of bubbles for a moment then turned back to her friends.

"We'd better get Sid," she said. "I can't stop him when he's in the water."

When they pulled up next to the pedalboat, Sid was still a little groggy but had untied the rope around his ankles.

"Climb on board," Durso said and offered a hand. Sid

stood with some difficulty and leaned into their boat. When he was finally seated Berdie immediately started washing the blood off his cheek.

"Don't leave their boat," Sid managed to say. "It's evidence."

Margaret looked at it for a moment, then moved to the back of the Bayliner. She reached into an open side compartment and removed the ski rope. "Let's see if I still remember what Tiny taught me." She made one end of the rope into a large loop and threw it outward toward the pedalboat a few feet away. By some miracle it landed over the steering bar and caught. Margaret tied the other end to a cleat on the back of the Bayliner and went back to the driver's seat.

"Won't Pete Feezel be surprised when he see's what we've got in tow," she said.

Berdie, who was looking around the boat with its shattered windscreen, ripped upholstery, and splintered fiberglass shook her head.

"I think he's going to be more surprised at what's towing it."

CHAPTER 40

...

The hard part had been finding the van. Grimes finally managed to track down a copy of the article Forstman had mentioned at the public library, and it did give the Second Street address. After that, the rest was easy. Grimes simply went into a nearby hardware store and picked up their $29.49 brown mechanics overalls, complete with a peaked hat that said At Your Service. The tool kit he borrowed from a locker in the hospital basement. For those important little touches Grimes made sure to pick up an oily rag, wipe it a few times across his pants, and leave it sticking out a good four inches from his back pocket.

Still, he was very cautious as he approached the van. He had chosen a time when everyone was either at lunch or napping, so there was no one on the porches nearby. Old people had a nasty habit of gossiping over trivia. The last thing he wanted was someone to inquire what had been wrong with the van to require a mechanic. There were still only a few cars parked nearby and not a single pedestrian. Twelve-thirty on a South Miami back street looked like 4:00 A.M. in a suburban shopping mall.

Grimes knocked on the side door first to make sure no one was in the van, then moved to the auxiliary generator compartment on the side by the gas intake. The two latches were screw-down types with grooves wide enough that they could be turned with quarters. He put his tool kit down and used a screwdriver instead, and in two minutes raised the compartment cover on its top hinge. Inside, the generator was set back six inches for air circulation, just enough room to wedge in the little package he had waiting in the bottom of the tool kit. But first he found the lead wires coming in from the left, took a nick out of the insulation on each one, and put the splice clamps in place. Then he stuck the powerful magnet with the hook to the inside of the van's steel skin and hung his little package in place. The only thing remaining was to plug the male leads from the red and green splice cable into the sockets on the side of the package, and he was done.

Just then, he took a glance to the right and noticed there was an old woman coming. He had forgotten about the goddamn dog walkers! She couldn't have been more than thirty yards away but fortunately the dog was taking its own good time with the shrubbery. So far, she hadn't seen him.

He fumbled for a second with the plugs, finally got them in place, and brought the cover down. There were still those two little screws but now Rover spotted something near the van and started tugging on the lead. Grimes only had time for one of them, but it would keep the cover from rattling. He pushed the hanging screw back in place and started in on it with the screwdriver. He was going too quickly and twice the tool slipped out of the wide groove, but finally he felt the screw grab and tighten. Then he quickly put the screwdriver back and closed the case. The woman was ten feet away, and struggling with the little dog to keep his nose out of the gutter. Grimes passed her in silence and kept walking. She hadn't noticed, he was sure of that. And now everything was all set. The moment the auxiliary generator was turned on in the van to power the internal sockets or for air-conditioning, the spark would set off his little package placed so dangerously close to the gas tank. Grimes grinned like a C student looking at an A on a test. Fortunately chemistry had always been one of his favorite subjects in medical school.

CHAPTER 41

...

Captain Diamond took all the commotion in front of his desk with a certain indifference. Like a bailiff waiting for the judge to arrive, he knew it wouldn't take more than a few crisp commands to quiet everyone. For the moment he was just listening.

In front of him Joe Durso was arguing with someone by the name of Pete Feezel, Margaret Binton was demanding they make immediate arrests, and two other septuagenarians, Sid Rossman and Berdie Mangione, were regaling each other and anyone else who would listen with their part in the day's activities. The place was a circus, and under normal circumstances Diamond would have thrown them all out on their ears. There was one undeniable fact, however, that raised the curious show from Grand Guignol to hard-core reality; the shattered pedalboat with its obvious pickup mechanism. It required that he get some coherent story out of them.

He brought his hand down on his battered desk and the noise it made stopped everyone in midsentence.

"Okay, one at a time," he said and pointed. "You first."

Margaret had the complete story out in ten minutes. She was so complete, in fact, that no one spoke after she sat back in the hard oak chair to await Diamond's response. There was, of course, only one thing he could do. He turned to his assistant, a full-bellied sergeant by the name of Wilkens, and told him to get cracking.

"I want to see this guy Franco and his employer, what's

169

his name . . . Forstman, and I want two search warrants, one for the hotel and one for this *Holidaze* boat. Also, pick up anyone on board and bring them in for questioning."

"And my clothes and stuff," Sid said. "It's all packed and waiting in room Eleven." Diamond nodded him out of the office, then, turned to Margaret with a pained expression on his face.

"Normally we have more lead time on these things and can plan them strategically. But your gangbusters approach leaves me no choice."

Margaret cleared her throat. "On the other hand, I daresay it's not often that you are handed such a golden opportunity without lifting a finger for it. Four unimpeachable witnesses willing to testify, the boat with the trick mechanism that picked up the drugs, incriminating fingerprints all over the place. Motive and method of a probable murder. What more could you ask for, especially in such a . . . shall we say . . . out of the way precinct. You should thank us, Captain Diamond. If you handle this right, it might get you out of here and into a bigger office with decent furniture." She shot him her most piercing stare. "Gangbusters, indeed!"

He grumbled a response that had, somewhere toward the end of it, a gruff-sounding "sorry." He motioned to Wilkens. "Get going. If we're in time we might get the whole operation."

"What about Doctor Grimes?" Sid asked after the door closed on Wilkens. "You haven't mentioned anything about him."

"What's to mention?" Diamond said. "All you have on him is that he recommends patients to Forstman, then visits them. That and he maybe changes bags during his visit."

"Not maybe," Sid said, "I'm sure of it."

"So what? It's not a crime. You want me to arrest a

guy, a doctor, because he owns a couple of bags. Maybe one is medicine and one is equipment."

Sid got red in the face. "You know goddamn well what was in that bag on the way out. How do you think they get the crack out without suspicion?"

"Look, I didn't say I'm not interested in Grimes. We're just not going to get him by raiding his office. He's too smart to have anything lying around. His lawyer would have him out in ten minutes and we'd look like a bunch of fools in front of any judge."

Diamond stood up and walked to the window. Along with his very used furniture, his view was less than first-rate. All he could see from his window was the side yard of the body repair shop. Still, it held his attention for a minute while he put things in sequence. "Grimes is clean. The only way to get him," he continued, "is to get the goods on one of the small fry, and then apply the screws. Franco or maybe even Forstman might go for a deal, especially if we get a hook into them deep enough. No, for the time being we have to leave Doctor Grimes alone."

"But it was his boat," Margaret said.

"I suppose you can prove that," Diamond said skeptically. "Even though *The Eternal Holidaze* is not registered in Florida, Delaware, or for that matter, on any computer in the United States."

"What?" Margaret looked surprised.

"When you called from Mr. Feezel's, I ran a quick check with some friends over at motor vehicles. Hey, it's easy to paint a name on the stern of a boat. You know what that means? She's probably out of Haiti or the Bahamas, and getting offshore records is about as easy as getting gum from the bottom of theater seats." He went back to his desk. "Much easier to lean on the other two."

"Three," Sid supplied. "Donna Slater is probably in on

it. And if she's not, you can get her on some other charge the way they use the food and medication in that place."

"That too," Diamond nodded. "I suppose it's all part of it. They used the old-age guest house as a cover and of course had to keep all the guests in line. Grimes tried to make sure they had the right kind to begin with."

"So what should the four of us do now?" Durso asked. "We were all sort of getting ready to go back to New York soon."

Diamond came back to his seat. "We'll need Rossman's testimony if we want to use an attempted murder charge. I still haven't figured out what we'll do with the Schecter part, maybe an autopsy. Then there's some loose ends. Better figure on another week down here minimum. Course you'll have to come back for any trial. Call me tomorrow and I'll fill you in on what's going on." He leaned back in his chair. "Hey, but what's the problem." He smiled. "You got your own mobile apartment, right? Won't cost you anything. And this is Miami. People pay a lot of money for a week down here."

"I can't see it," Margaret said. "It would be a lot cheaper to go to Albany this time of year. Same weather."

"Be patient," Diamond said. "It's supposed to break tomorrow or the next day. Forecast is for just a little more of this damp stuff, then sunny and hot. You'll have a week of perfect tropical climate—air-conditioning weather."

"At last," Berdie sighed.

CHAPTER 42

...

"So, what do you think?" Margaret asked the three others much later. "Should we reactivate the Dream-trippers Coach and Excursion Society or just relax for the rest of our vacation? I think we've earned it." She looked at her three friends, two sitting with her at the dinette, and Sid already in his bed. There was a bandage on his face where Franco had hit him, but otherwise he didn't seem to be too much the worse for wear. In front of Margaret was a cup of hot cocoa from the gas stove.

"Some vacation," Durso grumbled and looked out the window of the van. The dampness Captain Diamond had alluded to earlier in the day had congealed into a solid downpour. "The only thing worth sightseeing is an umbrella factory."

"I think we should make one more trip," Berdie said. "The one we never made. To Forstman's. Sounds like there's a whole lot of people there could use a day on the outside."

"What an absolutely wonderful idea," Margaret said. "Soon as the weather clears, we'll take everyone at Forstman's out. I should have thought of that." She finished her cocoa, got up, and moved slowly to the sink with the empty cup. It was late, and the four of them were already in their pajamas and robes. She put the cup in the sink, splashed some water on it, and heard the familiar sound of the battery-operated pump compressing more air to pressurize the system. "I'll do the dishes in the morning. I'm just so exhausted I couldn't do another thing. Good night." As she

173

started back toward the rear bedroom she looked at Sid. "You'll feel better in the morning. You're a real hero, you know." She leaned over and squeezed his hand. "And very brave."

"As I recall," he tried to smile, "I didn't have much choice in the matter."

CHAPTER 43

...

It stopped raining by the time Margaret came back next morning with the papers and fresh orange juice, but there was still no sign of a letup in the unseasonable weather. They had postponed any idea of a sightseeing trip because of the cold, and instead were planning just a quiet day in the van. The coffee was already waiting for her as she unloaded her packages on the table.

"Well," Sid asked. "You speak to Diamond?"

She sat down heavily and pushed the papers to one side.

"Sometimes I don't understand people," she began. "Yes, I spoke to him. I think he would have preferred it if we had let Franco kill Sid—then he could have pulled off his raids successfully. As it was, even though he assured me they got the warrants as quickly as they could, it wasn't quickly enough."

"What happened?" Durso asked.

"By the time they got to the boat it was empty. They checked for the underwater pickup device but all they found were the brackets for it. At the guest house the evidence was all gone also. They couldn't get rid of the smell of ether in the basement, but Diamond reminded me that odors can't be tagged as evidence in a court of law. He figures they must have dumped the chemicals in the canal. No sign of any cocaine, but that being worth probably close to half a million dollars, they probably hid it. It's not on the premises though. Diamond told me they checked everywhere. They brought Forstman in for questioning, but haven't charged him with anything yet. I guess they're waiting on Schecter's autopsy. Franco was booked on an attempted murder charge but was out on bail half an hour after they closed the cell door. Ms. Slater laughed in their faces when Diamond brought up her manipulation of the drugs. Needless to say no one has been convinced to implicate Doctor Grimes yet."

"But that's outrageous," Berdie said.

"Indeed," Margaret nodded and took a sip of hot coffee. "Diamond isn't even sure he can make the charges stick to Franco. 'You must remember,' he told me, 'it's just his word against your friend's.'"

"What about all the shots he took at us?" Berdie asked. "We've got three witnesses to that."

"Self-defense probably. He claimed we tried to run him down. In fact, from the looks of the pedalboat, Diamond thinks he has a pretty good case against us. Plus the gun is at the bottom of the canal." She finished the cup and got up to get some more. "Mind you, Diamond is not saying it's impossible to turn Franco, just difficult. He seems to think he doesn't have enough. The term he used was 'no smoking gun.'"

"You're right," Sid said angrily. "He probably would have liked a nice clean-cut drowning with a concrete anchor." He shook his head. "Isn't the law just wonderful."

"Anyway, they're talking to the guests at Forstman's now. Diamond hopes someone will have seen something. He's telling us to hold tight and keep the faith." Margaret lit a cigarette, inhaled deeply, and took another sip of coffee. "You think it's hot in here?"

Her question went unanswered. "What the hell does that mean?" Durso said. "Keep the faith."

"I suppose it means not to worry," Margaret said simply. "After all, Doctor Grimes is in sort of a tight spot now. He doesn't know what the police have on him or who's talking, so there's no telling what he'll do. Quite a few people can make his life miserable. Three of them are stonewalling." She looked around. "Then there's us." She finished her second cup and casually reached for the auxiliary generator switch. She had her hand on it before anyone spoke.

"Hey, what're you doing?" Berdie asked.

"You're not hot?"

"It's the coffee," Sid said. "And you just came in from carrying the papers. I don't think we need it."

Margaret frowned at him and hesitated for a second. "I guess you're right. The sun isn't even out." Slowly, she pulled her hand away. "And, I suppose, 'keep the faith' also translates roughly to 'be careful.'" She sat back and opened her sweater. "Which I trust, you'll all heed."

"I don't think we'll have a problem if we all stick together," Durso said. "Anyone for television?"

"Maybe after the paper," Sid said and reached for a piece of it. "Let's see what's happening at Hialeah."

Durso watched for a minute, then came over behind him. "How'd the Giants do?"

"Who cares?" Sid said. "I can never beat the point spread." He separated the papers and removed the racing section, giving Durso the main sports pages. In the process a single page fell and swooped down to the middle of the aisle. Margaret bent down to pick it up. No one noticed that she stayed that way for fifteen seconds, her body as immobile as if she'd been paralyzed. Slowly she brought the page up and laid it on the table in front of her.

"Good Lord," she breathed. "Look at this."

Berdie leaned over to where she was pointing, but all she could see was a tiny article about a fisherman having slipped into the water from one of the bridges over the Miami River in the Little Havana section. The accident victim was found with his legs all entwined with fish line when they recovered the body. The police figured it happened at night when he couldn't see his own gear and tripped into the river.

"So?" she asked.

"The name," Margaret said and pointed closer. "The name!" This time her voice was louder.

"Eduardo . . ."

"Diaz." Margaret finished it for her. "Eduardo Diaz, the mechanic on *The Eternal Holidaze*. Alvarez's friend." She looked up and into their eyes. "He's already begun."

CHAPTER 44

...

The phone rang by Forstman's elbow but he hesitated to pick it up. Even if he hadn't been pulled in for questioning the day before, his nerves were at a breaking point. He had never liked the idea of pulling the plug on Schecter, and now a bunch of cops were running through the guest house asking a lot of questions. Who knew what they'd come up with. Maybe they already had something and this call was that son of a bitch Diamond asking him to come back for another go-around. He lifted the receiver slowly and put it to his ear.

"Yeah?"

"Forstman?"

"Un hunh."

"This evening, six o'clock at the boat. Bring the others. We gotta talk." Forstman was about to say something when he heard the click from the other end. The entire call had taken all of five seconds. Good, he thought, now we'll get everything straight.

...

Margaret double-parked the Winnebago in front of the police station and the four of them rushed inside. This time when they gave their names to the desk sergeant they were ushered into Diamond's office right away. The captain looked up to find Margaret thrusting a news clipping at him.

"Yeah, Diaz," he said. "So? It's out of my precinct."

179

"Diaz is the man who gave me the connection between Grimes and the boat."

Diamond sat back and said nothing for a moment. He seemed to be concentrating on a small round coffee stain on the edge of the desk. Finally he looked at the four of them and shook his head slowly.

"I don't like it. We didn't have Forstman and Slater and Franco Richmond twenty minutes before a lawyer appeared on their behalf. The bail set on Richmond was twenty thousand and half an hour later the bond was posted. Someone wanted them free quickly."

"It's to keep them quiet," Margaret said.

"Yeah, but the question is, how persuasive will he get."

"That's pretty clear." She pointed to the clipping.

"The three of them?" Diamond said.

"For starters."

Diamond reached for the phone and asked for a number. In a few seconds he was through.

"Wilkens," he said. "Anything yet from the guests?" Margaret and the others watched as he frowned. "How about the tap?" This time he must have hit something because he rocked forward and pulled over a piece of paper.

"Could you repeat that." Margaret and her friends leaned closer. "That was all? Okay, thanks." He hung up and studied the paper.

"Grimes?" Durso asked.

"No name, but whoever it is put something on for tonight on the boat." He picked up the phone again. "Which means I'll need ears inside the boat. Yeah," he said into the mouthpiece, "get me the equipment sergeant." He looked up at them and smiled. "We'll get a little bug that's good around water. Then we'll send Wilkens back in on the same warrant."

"What should we do?" Sid asked.

Diamond said nothing for a moment, then shrugged. "I don't know, there's a good movie playing over at the Triplex."

"Hey," the four of them said at once.

"Forget it," Diamond frowned. "There's no way in hell you're coming with me tonight."

CHAPTER 45

...

They had to pull in to their old spot by the canal and use the glasses. Given the fact that they had brought everything to a head, they all agreed it was quite unsatisfactory to have been left out at the last moment. Still, they got to see the six policemen fan out into the neighboring parked boats, and the fast unmarked police Sea Ray pull into a nearby slip.

By six o'clock everyone was there except Grimes. Even the bodyguard Alvarez had mentioned had popped up on deck one time. The four New Yorkers passed the glasses back and forth and grumbled the whole time. The only good note was that the weather was finally warming up. The clouds had dissipated, and the sky looked clear. Everything was quite still, so calm, in fact, that Sid and Durso heard the little rhythmic splashing of the oars before anyone saw the rubber dinghy turn the corner of the canal. In the boat was a lone figure in a jogging outfit. For some reason he had chosen to arrive without noise because in the stern of the dinghy a small motor looked ready for use. He quietly tied his bow line to one of the stern rails of the Trumpy and swiveled himself on board. In his hand he carried what looked like an overnight case.

Margaret happened to be holding the glasses when the figure walked quietly up the port wing and turned into the wheelhouse. It was dark enough so that it was difficult to see his face.

"I don't know, it could be Grimes," Margaret said softly and handed the glasses to Sid. "What do you think?"

But by the time he got the focus adjusted for his eyes, the man was inside. Sid scanned the area for fifty yards on either side, but nothing was moving. "Now what?" he asked.

Margaret sighed. "Canasta, I suppose. You heard what Diamond said. We're out of it."

■ ■ ■

"Now what?" Wilkens whispered into the radio. He was the closest of the policemen on foot. He had found a hiding place on *Daddy's Toy* right next to *The Eternal Holidaze* and had seen the arrival of the little dinghy.

"Hold tight," Diamond said from inside the Sea Ray. "I've got them on the wire. I'll let you know when to move." He turned down the volume on the Wilkens earphone and turned up the sound on the other one. He was just in time to catch the greeting. It came in with a little static, but was clear enough to understand.

"Jesus Christ, where'd you come from?"

"The water. Just a precaution. We all here?"

"Yeah, all here and goddamn anxious about what's going down."

"I'll tell you everything," the raspy voice said, "in due time. Right now I don't want any uninvited company. Willie, take the wheel. Franco, pull the lines. I want to be past Fisher Island and out Government Cut in ten minutes."

Diamond leaned forward and peered out the window. Someone started moving around the stern of the big boat. Suddenly he heard a low crackle in his left ear.

"Captain, they're taking off. What do I do?"

Diamond made a snap decision. If he sent them in now he'd have nothing.

"Hang tight, Wilkens, I'll handle it."

The bow line was cast off at the same time that the

Trumpy's big diesel kicked into life. They gave it only twenty seconds of warmup before they put the boat in gear. *The Eternal Holidaze* moved into the middle of the canal and turned left, in the direction of the outlets to the Atlantic. Tagging behind like a little lost heifer was the rubber dinghy, still tied on a short lead to the stern rail.

Diamond motioned to the officer from the harbor patrol at the controls of the Sea Ray. They waited until the Trumpy was around the bend, then headed slowly after them. When they emerged into Biscayne Bay, the big boat was maybe a half mile away and headed south. Diamond didn't want to blow it by following too closely but the transmission from the Trumpy was coming in indistinctly. There were big patches of static that Diamond couldn't hear through. He motioned to the driver, and the Sea Ray put on a little speed. They were running without lights, so the chances were lessened that they would be spotted. There was no moon and Diamond knew that out past the shore lights there'd be even less to see by. They pulled up to within about a quarter mile and slightly abeam where they had no trouble keeping pace. At that spot, the little bug in the Trumpy's cabin was working beautifully. Unfortunately, there wasn't anything to hear yet. Diamond figured the real show wouldn't begin until they were past Fisher Island and into the ocean. He was hoping Grimes's name would come up and then if they were real lucky, maybe he'd say something incriminating that they could catch on tape. On the other hand, if Grimes started threatening, Diamond was close enough to come charging in with lights and sirens to discourage anything serious from happening. That's the way he had it figured.

■ ■ ■

Birdie was the one who noticed when the boat started pulling out. She was not a cardplayer and was sitting in the driver's seat listening to some Mantovani string piece on WKOSY. She was trying to hum along when she glanced over across the canal and spotted the boat as it was straightening out.

"Hey," she said out loud. "They're taking off."

Sid looked out the dinette window and watched as the boat started down the canal. Four minutes later he saw the police boat move after them.

"I don't suppose you have any bright ideas?"

Margaret shook her head. "I'm afraid not. This is one we have to wait out. I have a feeling," she said throwing down the club deuce, "that it's going to be a long night."

"A long hot night," Berdie added and reached for the generator switch. In the darkness of the front seat, her hand found a switch and pushed it. At first there was a slow humming noise, and then quickly the exhaust fan over the stove picked up speed and started sucking air out of the Winnebago.

"That's a good idea, Berdie," Margaret said. "Get some of this stale air out of here."

"I was thinking of air-conditioning," she answered. "I hit the wrong switch."

"There are six cops across the canal and we're not supposed to be here," Sid said. "The fan'll do fine. I'll open a window."

Berdie shrugged and sank back into the soft seat. In a minute she was back humming with Mantovani.

■ ■ ■

The Eternal Holidaze passed through Government Cut and kept going straight. She picked up speed when she hit the open water and started planing, making over fifteen knots. Even though the Trumpy had been built for gracious cruising and not for ocean pounding, the old boat handled the three-foot waves well. She kicked up a large frothy wake that would have been easy to follow, even in the moonless night, but Diamond wasn't going to risk it. He wanted the Sea Ray farther abeam and downwind, both so that the sound of his motor wouldn't carry and so he wouldn't be silhouetted against the shore lights. Then they kept pace, listening carefully on the earphones for what was going on. There was still nothing of interest coming from the cabin where the bug was, not unless you called a lot of complaining about the bumpy ride important. They kept on for ten minutes until the horizon behind them was an indistinct blur of lights, and then suddenly *The Eternal Holidaze* stopped.

Diamond almost missed it. He was doing fifteen knots and only realized the change in speed when he started to pick up a lot of static on the earphones. Diamond told the driver to double back and ease in to a little under half a mile. He was confident that the Sea Ray was fairly undetectable in the open ocean with its dark blue hull and without any lights showing. As they got closer, he started picking up new sounds from the bug, sounds of arguing. When he got the clarity he wanted, he told the driver to cut the motor. The Sea Ray glided to a halt and immediately began bobbing between the waves. Diamond, not accustomed to the motion of small boats in the ocean, held onto the dashboard with one hand and pressed the earphone closer with the other. He stayed like that for the next five minutes while the five people in the other boat sorted out their differences.

There were a lot of raised voices, but as far as Diamond could tell, it was all about extortion, not death threats. They started at half a million and were working their way down when Grimes, or the man everyone called "doctor," excused himself to go get something from the wheelhouse. When he was gone Diamond heard one of the remaining four suggest that they take no less than three hundred and fifty thousand to keep the lid on. This was good stuff, Diamond figured, all going on tape. He could certainly throw an attempted blackmail charge on any of them to twist their arms further.

He was straining to hear more when another, different sound came to him. But this one came through both ears, and the strangeness of the sensation had him befuddled. Then he realized that the bug was picking up the dinghy's motor at the same time that he was getting it across the water. It took him only a few seconds to realize just what that meant. Unfortunately the people in the boat were not as clever, or maybe they were still working on what to do with their part of the three hundred and fifty thousand.

"Christ!" Diamond said immediately and tore off the earphone. "Kick this son of a bitch up and get us over there . . . full throttle." He held on tighter as the Sea Ray roared into life and shot forward. The sound of their combined 600-horsepower motors completely masked the little dinghy's, but Diamond had already made the decision to go for the Trumpy. They were halfway there when the sky in front of them lit up with an orange fireball and the shock wave of the explosion tore the canvas canopy over their heads. Instinctively, the driver next to Diamond threw the wheel over and cut back. They were over a quarter of a mile away and still they didn't escape being hit by a few pieces of charred wood and splinters of glass. The rain of debris continued for ten seconds. When it stopped, Diamond pointed and they turned back. He glanced down and saw by the dashboard clock that it was exactly six twenty-one.

The explosion had been designed to do two things, kill everyone on board, and sink the boat. It had been a combination of high explosives packed inside a steel cylinder, which was then packed inside several quart containers of gasoline. When it went off in the back of the wheelhouse, the steel of the cylinder shot through the old wood of the boat like a fusillade of machine-gun fire. The explosion of gasoline followed the pathways created by the shattering shrapnel and raked the inside of the saloon with fire. The bottom part of the cylinder tore straight down and fractured the keel, basically cutting the boat in half. By the time the embers had stopped floating back down to the water, the Trumpy lay like a child's toy after the family dog has chewed it. Water poured in through the gaping holes in the bottom and the added weight was all that was needed to sever the two halves. In no time, the stern, with its heavy motors, sank. Two minutes later, the bow section followed it. Diamond arrived just in time to hear the last gurgle of trapped air make it back to the surface. Unfortunately, it was the only noise to be heard.

At first, the two men in the Sea Ray were too stunned to speak. Diamond had been to many murder scenes, but this was different. Pyrotechnics aside, he had never been witness to the instant disappearance of an object the size of a small ranch house. Its only remnants were splintered bits of wood, mostly light paneling, and galley junk. Diamond looked on the wrecked scene and grimaced. He turned on his boat's search light, but even before he swept the surface with its beam he knew there would be no survivors, not from that explosion. After a few moments he picked up the radio in front of him.

"Headquarters, this is Captain Diamond. Alert the Coast Guard that we've had an explosion and a sinking. Four deaths. Ask them to send someone out and also monitor the inlets for a small black rubber dinghy with one man on board. Stop and detain. We'll circle and try to locate him from our position. The wreckage is approximately three to four miles due east of Government Cut. We'll drop a flare. Over." The driver unpacked one of the floating flares and tossed it overboard. Then he sat back down and waited for Diamond to tell him a direction out of the fetid and overpowering atmosphere of burning diesel oil and charred wood.

"It would be stupid for him to go back through the inlet," Diamond said. "He could beach that little dinghy anywhere, Lummus Park, Pier Park, the whole strip in front of Collins Avenue. Sensible too; he could melt away in the pedestrian traffic."

"So?"

"What the hell, we'll give it a try. Pier Park, it's closest."

The driver nodded and headed the Sea Ray west. They got there in five minutes, but Diamond had been right. They found the little dinghy nosed into the beach with its stern awash in the surf. There was no one on the beach and no one they could see in the thin little park.

"I can't bring her in," the driver said. "The surf's too high."

"No matter," Diamond said, "I'll get him tomorrow. I know who he is."

CHAPTER 46

...

It hit the eleven o'clock news, but by that time all the people in the Winnebago were asleep. They caught it the next morning when Margaret came back with the paper and more fresh orange juice. It was, finally, a gorgeous South Florida day. The temperature was already in the eighties and the sky was cloudless. But the weather was not the only thing on page one.

The *Herald* played it up big. You could tell the editor had wanted a picture, but the best thing they could come up with was a snapshot of a similar-sized Trumpy. The story had the time of the explosion at 6:21, when several hotel guests on the strip called in to report it. An unnamed police source was quoted as having said the explosion was drug-related and that the number of unconfirmed deaths stood at four. No one as yet had been arrested.

Margaret put the paper down slowly and looked around at her friends. The three others had varying expressions on their faces but they were variations on a basic theme . . . fear. Without saying anything, Margaret started the Winnebago up and edged it back onto the road.

"Where are you going?" Sid asked.

"To make sure Grimes is behind bars. They've had all night to get him."

...

The police station was a mess of reporters trying to get more out of Diamond, but so far he wasn't cooperating. When Margaret and the three others pushed their way in he was repeating for maybe the third time that they were still investigating the explosion and that no arrests had been made. He spotted the four New Yorkers and motioned them into his office, leaving the reporters with a few "no further comments" to play with. As soon as the door closed behind him, Margaret started in.

"What was that, no arrests have been made? What about Grimes?"

Diamond looked as if he hadn't seen ten minutes of sleep in the last twenty-four hours and moved about as energetically. He pointed to the few wooden chairs around his desk then tumbled into his own. He levered himself back, took a deep breath, and closed his eyes.

"Well?" Margaret said.

"He didn't do it." Diamond said. He opened his eyes but didn't bother to sit back up.

"What? But we saw him at the boat," Sid said.

Diamond looked at the four of them, then swung up slowly. "I'm not even going to ask why you were there, and let's forget for the moment that you couldn't have been closer than a hundred yards." He looked directly at Sid. "Are you prepared to swear in court that it was Doctor Grimes . . . without any doubt? Because I was there too, and so were Sergeant Wilkens and six others, and none of us can say we got a good look at his face."

Sid turned to Margaret and frowned. "You saw him, didn't you?"

She hesitated for a few seconds. "Yes, it was him. I saw him in the binoculars."

"Well," Diamond said slowly. "That gives us one hell of a problem. Now you tell me how one man could be in two places at one time, two places, I might add, over five miles apart." He looked from one to the other and smiled. "I'm afraid it won't stand up. Even a putz of a defense attorney would destroy that testimony. Dark night, over one hundred yards away . . . let me ask you, Mrs. Binton, do you ever wear glasses?"

"Well, maybe only for reading."

"Uh hunh." Diamond nodded. "Would it interest you to know that Doctor Grimes was in his office on Alton Road all afternoon right up to six-twenty P.M.?"

"What?"

"And that he has a witness, a heavy-duty witness in fact, to the last hour and a half of that. Judge Robert Thomas of the Broward County Surrogate Court. And Judge Thomas stood right next to him, shook his hand, and said good-bye at six-twenty. Judge Thomas, by the way, does not need glasses for reading."

"I can't believe it," Margaret said and looked at her friends.

"I don't either," Captain Diamond said, "but there it is. When I went to pick Grimes up this morning at his home he had it all prepared. I immediately went to speak to Judge Thomas and he confirmed what Grimes had said." Diamond made a fist and brought it down on the desk top. "Dammit, I heard them on the bug, I heard them call the guy that came on board a doctor, and from the way they were talking, I know it was someone they were familiar with. I went over every inch of tape, but there isn't anything there to pin on Grimes. Someone has to shake Thomas. I tried for an hour but I can't figure it."

Margaret reached into her handbag and pulled out her pack of Camels. She left them on the desk top out of intuition. This was going to take a while. She found the lighter, lit the Camel, and inhaled deeply.

"In his office?" she asked. "What was Judge Thomas doing there?"

"He was a patient of Grimes's. Had been ever since a

mild heart attack he suffered a year ago. Grimes called him the day before yesterday and told him he thought it was time he saw him. His last checkup had been a month before."

"Well, that's a start," Margaret said. "Grimes was setting him up. His most respected patient, I'll bet. Normally you don't bring a patient in on a day's notice. Was the month time span normal?"

"Just about. Thomas had an appointment already scheduled for the next week, but Grimes moved it up."

Margaret nodded. "Figures. What time was Thomas's appointment?"

"Four forty-five."

"He arrived on time?"

"A few minutes early. He checked it on his watch and also on the big clock in the waiting room."

Margaret closed her eyes. She stayed that way, holding the cigarette in front of her lips. Occasionally she'd take a tiny puff.

"What clock?"

"I don't know. Thomas said there was a big clock, an electric clock, on the wall facing where he was sitting. It said four-forty when he sat down."

"Umm." Margaret motioned. "Go on."

"Doctor Grimes comes out at four-fifty and greets Thomas, says he's running late, and tells him to just make himself comfortable. There is still one other patient before the judge. Thomas opens a magazine and sits back." Here Diamond opened a little notebook on the desk and turned a page. "At five-ten, the other patient is called in, and Grimes once again apologizes to Thomas for the delay."

"No nurse?" Margaret asked.

"No nurse, receptionist left at a little after five. Anyway, these delays seem to be fairly standard for most doctors, but Thomas is pretty annoyed nonetheless. Finally, at five-thirty Grimes comes out, says he's just finishing up, and would Thomas please undress in room one and put on the examining robe. He does that and continues to wait."

"And removes his watch?"

"Yes. How'd you know?"

"Continue." Margaret took a final puff and crushed out the cigarette.

"So at a quarter of six Grimes comes in and calls him into the examining room. One hour after his appointment."

"How does he know the time?"

"Another big clock in room one. Grimes examines him, gives him a cardiogram, etc., etc., and at six-ten tells him to get dressed."

"Has he left the room at all?" Margaret asked.

"Yes, for no more than a minute to get another roll of paper for the machine. Keep in mind it's now six-ten and as far as we're concerned, Grimes is on board *The Eternal Holidaze* and somewhere near Government Cut. At six-fifteen they meet in Grimes's office. How does Thomas know? The desk clock says six-fifteen, the Muzak station breaks in now and then with the time, and Thomas's own watch confirms it. It's a Rolex and Grimes says he's got one too and swears by it. They talk for five minutes, Grimes gives him a pretty clean bill of health, and Thomas leaves. On the way out he glances at the clock, which says six-twenty. He is unshakable about that. You will recall that the explosion occurred one minute later at a time when the murderer was escaping in a rubber dinghy." Diamond leaned back again and smiled. "Now, you tell me how he did it."

Margaret shook her head. "Well, the unfortunate fact is it doesn't matter. I think I can tell you how it's done, but Thomas isn't going to change a word of his story. You know of any juror that's going to buck the testimony of a judge?"

"Still, I'm curious," Diamond said.

Margaret leaned forward and plucked out another cigarette. "You'll need to ask the judge two more questions."

Diamond referred to his notes again and brought the phone over. In a few moments he had Thomas back on the line. He raised his eyebrows toward Margaret.

"You said pretty clean bill of health. Ask him was his heart rate a little high." She waited while Diamond put the question. In a moment he nodded. "And did Grimes check it once again before Thomas left just to make sure." A moment later Diamond nodded again, but this time he had a puzzled look on his face. "You can hang up," she said. "That's it."

"Okay," Diamond said. "I'm waiting."

Margaret exhaled a cloud of smoke in the direction of the window and straightened her dress. "The clocks were interesting. The one on his desk was the easy one; it was set a half hour in advance to begin with. The problem was with the two others. I might add that neither of them was there when I visited, so he put them in specially for Thomas. I wouldn't be surprised if they were either rigged to run fast or if there was a way for them to gain a minute every now and then, say by the simple device of a hole cut out of the paneling behind them from which to reset them every few minutes. The paneling you can check but I'd be surprised if those same clocks are still there. Thomas comes in and sees the waiting room clock at the right time, then as he waits and waits, it gains more and more minutes against real time. When he's called in to undress at five-thirty on the waiting room clock it's probably actually five-ten. It's only natural, when you're waiting and annoyed, time seems to stretch out. Grimes was clever enough to make use of a basic human reaction."

"What about Thomas's watch?" Berdie asked.

"If you were staring at a big clock in front of you, would you bother with your watch?"

Berdie shook her head slowly.

"The clock in room number one is set to conform with the waiting room clock, at five-thirty, but as soon as he's there, that one also gains time, maybe another five minutes. Finally, when Grimes finishes the examination he's probably picked up a half hour. The Muzak was also a nice touch. He probably recorded it the day before and just played it a half hour ahead of schedule. You said it was only playing in his office?"

Diamond nodded.

"Then came the master touch, the fiddle with Thomas's watch." She regarded the smoke rise from the end of her cigarette. "The problem here was more complicated. He had to set the watch ahead a half hour, have Thomas look at it for confirmation, then somehow, set it back again. It wouldn't do for him to discover the half hour discrepancy later that evening."

Diamond interrupted. "So when he left the room for the roll of paper he set Thomas's watch ahead?"

"That's right, and when he took his pulse just before Thomas left, which was after he had confirmed the time on his watch, Grimes set it back to the correct time. I'm pretty sure with one hand on your wrist pressing on an artery you wouldn't notice that the other, steadying your watch for a second count, was also quickly changing the setting. I'm sure Grimes did it in a casual gesture, something like this." She parked her cigarette in an ashtray, then leaned over and put both of her hands on Diamond's wrist. After fifteen seconds of looking at his watch she released her grip and sat back.

"Pulse rate of sixty-four. Not bad for a man your age." Diamond brought his hand up and looked. His watch had gained over an hour. "Did you feel it?" she asked.

Diamond laughed and shook his head at the same time. "Very good. I've got to hand it to you, and you're not even a doctor."

"And that's how he established his alibi. When Thomas left it was probably only five-fifty. That gave Grimes ten minutes to get to the little dinghy and paddle what must have been only a few blocks to *The Eternal Holidaze*. He murders four people and there's no way you can pin it on him." She retrieved her cigarette and took a final puff. "Not that I had any love for his business partners."

"Still, I hate to see him walk," Diamond said.

"Me too."

Diamond shook his head. "The only way we're going to get Grimes now is to have the incredible luck to catch him with that last shipment Franco retrieved. But we don't even know where to look for the stuff. We can't tail him twenty-four hours a day."

Margaret crushed out her second cigarette and put the pack back in her handbag. "Under the circumstances," she said, "I guess you won't be needing us. Franco is gone . . . so is Forstman." She looked at her friends. "I think we'd all feel better if we went back to New York soon. Maybe even tomorrow. I think the four of us have had quite enough excitement for one trip." She stood up. "The only thing left is to explain to the judge how it was done and hope he changes his story. Otherwise, I'm afraid you're right, Grimes is going to get away with it. Six murders." She stood up. "We just don't want to be around in case he decides to wipe the slate clean and make it an even ten."

CHAPTER 47

...

"We promised ourselves, remember," Berdie said. "One last excursion as the Dream-trippers Coach and Excursion Society, and we agreed it would be for the guests at Forstman's. Now, more than ever, they need a diversion to get their minds off their troubles."

"Berdie's right," Margaret said. "Why don't we go now?" Durso grumbled something about maybe spending their last day at the beach, but they all shouted him down. "Okay, okay," he finally agreed. "But promise me . . . not the Seaquarium."

For the first time in a week, they put on the air-conditioning on the way to Forstman's, running it off the motor and battery. It was getting to be a scorcher and the inside of the van seemed to trap the heat. When they arrived, they turned everything off, and the four of them went inside the guest house.

Things had greatly changed in the last forty-eight hours. It was obvious that some of the guests had already left. However, the doors were open and a few of the remaining guests were sunning themselves on the porch. Mrs. Epping was one of them. After telling Sid how shocked and saddened she was at the news, she explained that they were actually doing very nicely taking care of themselves. A cooking group had been organized, as well as a shopping contingent, and they were in the process of developing a work schedule for the other tasks. She confided in them that she'd never been so pleasantly busy in the last five years. When Sid offered the sightseeing tour she went to round up some others. In no time she had seven more, including Mrs. Kass, and the entire group marched out to the van.

"Where to?" Margaret asked, starting up the big motor.

"The Lincoln Road Mall," this from the back, and also "Miami Nursery" from Mrs. Kass.

Margaret slowly pulled out. She usually gave the seat next to her to one of the guests, and for this trip it was offered to Mrs. Epping. After a few minutes on the road, Margaret started up a conversation.

"How long will you stay on?" she asked. "Surely the guest house won't stay open very much longer."

Mrs. Epping shrugged and looked out the side window at a young woman pushing a pram. "I don't know. Maybe a week. It's fun now, but I can see it getting quite wearing. It's the little things that spoil it. Shopping and cooking we all know; but repairing the leaky faucet in the second floor john, or replacing the two fluorescent lights on the top landing that went out a couple of days ago . . ." she shook her head, "that's the hard part. We're all okay around a hot stove, but none of us wants to tackle live electricity or a plumbing job."

"I know what you mean," Margaret said. "That stuff frightens me. If it weren't for my superintendent in New York, I'd spend all my nights in the dark. I'd been spoiled, see, it had always been my late husband's job to change the light bulbs."

After another few minutes of chatting, Mrs. Epping pointed out the front window. "I think that's the nursery coming up."

"So it is," Margaret said and slowed down. She raised her voice behind her. "Are we all going in? If anyone wants to sit outside, I can put on the auxiliary air-conditioning for you." She waited, but no one took up her option. "Okay," she said, and turned off the motor. "Let's meet back here in an hour. I think there'll be time to go to the Lincoln Mall after that." She watched as the people began filing out the side door but was slow to join them. Something was sticking in her craw, but somehow she couldn't get a fix on it. She locked the door behind her and followed the group inside. "Damn," she muttered. "What was it?"

After the nursery they all had lunch in a little restaurant nearby and then headed off to the mall. The seven guests were like little kids in a video arcade. They wanted to look into every store, point out every new product, try on new sunglasses, and hats. They even went after the two- and three-dollar giftshop junk. After an hour, Margaret and her friends were exhausted keeping track of them. At four o'clock she managed to round them all up and bring them back to the van. From there it was only a short trip to Forstman's.

"Lucky, we just barely made it with the gas," Margaret said as she turned off the motor in front of their gate. "Now you're sure you'll be all right?"

Mrs. Kass beamed. "Absolutely, Margaret. I can't wait to use my new pen and pencil set." She held out the clear vinyl case with the two slender white writing instruments placed side by side with the words Miami Beach written on each one. Margaret reached out and looked at it a little longer than one would expect for a $3.95 purchase. "You all have been just so nice," Mrs. Kass added. "I wish we could do something for you."

"Ah, but you just have," Margaret said and handed the writing set back. "Do you mind if we come in for a moment?"

"What's up?" Sid asked as the four New Yorkers followed the seven others up the steps.

"Just a hunch," Margaret said softly. "Diamond told me he had this place combed for that last parcel of cocaine Franco made off with but couldn't find it. I can't imagine Forstman risked leaving the hotel with it. After all it must have taken Franco longer to swim back to the hotel than it would have taken me to get to a telephone and call the police." She smiled. "They had to hide it in the hotel and now I think I know where." This time she actually laughed. "Quite clever too. Everyone always looks in places that could have an empty space carved out . . . books or false table bases, things like that. No one ever looks for the obvious things that already have the spaces."

Berdie was doing her best to keep pace with the others. "Like where?" she asked, puffing.

But Margaret didn't answer directly. "You know, the human brain is a funny thing the way it makes associations. Mrs. Kass showed me a quite ordinary writing set and immediately I saw it. Before that I had all the information from Mrs. Epping, but it just didn't register."

In the main hallway they caught up with the others. Margaret took a deep breath. "Would you mind," she asked Mrs. Epping, "showing me the two fluorescent lights that against all odds went out together on the same day, the day Franco came back and warned Forstman the game was up? One thing Oscar always said was that we should switch to fluorescents because they rarely went out."

Berdie's eyes widened at the same time Sid slapped his thigh.

"Goddamn," he shouted.

"Wait a minute," Durso interrupted. "You can't open a fluorescent tube just like that and stick stuff in it."

"You can if you've prepared for it in advance and have two dummy tubes waiting," Margaret said. "It's a perfect hiding place. During the day the fluorescent lights wouldn't be on and the bogus ones wouldn't be noticed. At night it's just a couple of blown bulbs. But I'll bet each one can hold a couple of pounds of cocaine." She turned back to Mrs. Epping. "Which way, dear?"

The other woman led the way up to the top landing while Sid scouted up a ladder. Shortly he had unscrewed the cover on the outer case and was looking at two quite ordinary four-foot bulbs. But as soon as he removed the first one, his face broke out into a grin. "This thing weighs a ton," he said and handed it to Durso. "Same for the other one." He came down off the ladder.

"I think," Margaret said, "Captain Diamond would be delighted with the Dream-trippers Coach and Excursion Society's last day of operations." She picked one up. "I suppose we should take them over right away."

"Almost right away," Durso said. "Aren't you forgetting something."

"Like what?" Margaret said frowning.

"Gasoline."

■ ■ ■

The nearest station was on Dade Boulevard, which they made without problem. Margaret pulled in out of the twilight shadows onto the bright-lit tarmac and turned off the ignition. Durso jumped out the side door and opened the gas cap, then brought over the nozzle of the nearest pump.

"Ten dollars?" he called.

"Be a sport," Margaret shouted back. "Make it twenty. No telling how far we'll have to drive to sell this thing." Durso pulled back the trigger and locked it in place. Then he leaned against the van and waited. Just my luck, he thought after a minute of watching. The slowest pump in Florida.

With the ignition and motor off, and the windows

closed, the inside of the van soon got as hot as an oven. It was a little past five o'clock, but it was still in the eighties. Margaret opened her window but it didn't help.

"How much longer?" she shouted out the window, but Durso was no longer looking at the gas dial. His attention had strayed to the side of the van, and leisurely down to the auxiliary generator compartment. Right away he noticed that one of the screws was not engaged, which was peculiar. When he took a step over to check it, he saw the scratch marks around the other one, which was also peculiar. The few times he had checked inside the compartment he always used a quarter to turn the big screws. He fished in his pocket, removed a coin and started screwing the loose screw back in. After one or two turns his curiosity got the better of him and he reversed his motion.

Margaret, inside the van, couldn't take the heat any more. She leaned forward and reached for the auxiliary generator switch. For all she knew it would take another ten minutes until Durso finished and paid and by then she'd probably faint. She leaned as far as she could go, but her seat belt was still buckled and her finger came four inches short of reaching the button. She rocked back, unhooked the belt, and slid to her right. As she leaned forward again, Berdie, who was sitting next to her in the front seat, said, "I'll do it," and leaned forward herself, pushing the button.

"No," Margaret said. "Not the radio, the generator. I'm dying of the heat."

"That's a bad idea right now," Sid called from the dinette behind her. "The generator's right next to the gas intake and who knows if it gives out a spark . . ."

Margaret hesitated for just a second. "Why would they put it so close if it wasn't safe?" She leaned forward again but was halted by the shout from outside. It wasn't so much a shout as a terrified cry. She'd never heard a voice with so much panic in it before, and the voice, strangely, belonged to Durso.

"What the. . . ?" Sid started, and rushed out the door. Margaret was close behind, followed by Berdie. When they swung around the van and found Durso, his face was as white as the lettering on the pump. All he could do at first was point, but as Margaret stuck her face close to the opening, he finally came to life.

"No, don't. It's a bomb! God knows how long it's been there."

"A what?"

"A goddamn bomb. Four sticks of dynamite taped together and hanging on a magnet . . . connected to the generator. All it would have taken was pushing the button."

Margaret felt her knees get weak and she had to lean against the pump. "Oh my God," she said, "I almost blew us sky high."

"More than once," Sid recalled. "It's a good thing the weather's been so cold."

Durso very carefully turned off the pump and removed the nozzle. He moved as though he were walking on eggs, and only breathed easier when the gas cap was back on. The pump read $18.67.

"Don't pay yet," Margaret said abruptly. She had straightened up. Her face still looked drained, but there was an angry edge to it. "I want to figure this out and I need a few minutes." She nodded in the direction of the gas attendant busy with another car. "Don't say anything."

"I'm not getting back in that van if that's what you have in mind," Durso said.

Berdie took an involuntary step toward him. "Me neither."

Margaret looked at both of them, then took a few steps over and sank down on a bench at the side of the station.

She folded her hands in her lap and looked straight ahead. Most anybody glancing her way would have thought she was waiting patiently for a bus, but Sid knew better. He came over cautiously and sat down next to her.

"What are you thinking?" he asked.

She frowned slightly but didn't say anything. Her eyes remained fixed at a point about ten feet in front of the Winnebago. The only things that moved were her thumbs, patting against each other rhythmically in her folded hands. For three or four minutes she stayed that way while the four of them watched. Finally, the gas station attendant broke the silence.

"Hey, you finished or what?" he called. Durso blinked and reached into his pocket for the twenty.

Margaret took a deep breath and turned toward Sid. "I won't need you either," she said. "Not in the van. But I will need some help"—she looked over at the clock on the front of the station—"in an hour."

"Help, for what?" he asked.

Margaret's brown eyes held Sid's with a look he had never seen before. Their intensity made him feel strangely uncomfortable.

"He's killed six so far, and been inches away from making it ten. The man is psychotic and very dangerous. It's time he paid."

"Go to Diamond with it," Sid said softly, "like we planned."

She shook her head sadly. "What can he do? He's bound by laws and procedures that make my head spin. It's all come to this, Diamond said so himself, Grimes is going to walk."

"So?"

"So," Margaret fumbled in her handbag for a moment and finally removed a pencil and some paper. "Here's an address I want the three of you at by six o'clock. It's not far. I'll be parked by the curb. Stay in the darkness until you hear the stove exhaust fan go on, then walk over by the front door and wait for me. I should be coming out in a short time."

Sid looked shocked. "You getting back in that van?"

"I have to," she said. "It's the only way. I've got to get back in it, and drive it, and talk to someone."

"To whom?" Sid looked hopelessly lost. "And about what?"

"About friendship, old-time friendship," Margaret said and got up. "With Renan Alvarez, to whom I suspect it means a lot." She took a few steps toward the van, then turned back toward Sid. "Don't let me down. Talk to Berdie and Durso. I can't tell you how important it is that you're there."

"But Margaret, there's a bomb on board."

"And has been probably for quite some time." She flashed him a weak little smile. "Don't worry, I'm not going to be needing any auxiliary power this evening."

CHAPTER 48

...

She found Alvarez on board his boat right next to the empty Trumpy slip. He had been down below, slightly red-eyed and drinking from a pint bottle of Canadian Club. Eduardo's funeral had been that morning. She turned down a drink, then spent the next fifteen minutes talking softly to him. When she was finished, he followed her onto the dock, then over to the van. When they parted several minutes later, she leaned over and squeezed his arm.

"Thank you," she said. "I feel so responsible for what happened to Eduardo."

He looked up at her with eyes that still held a measure of pain. Then he shrugged. "Hey, he shoulda known better. It was a bad scene from the beginning."

Margaret nodded slowly, then turned and got back in the van. "I won't need to tell you what happens," she called down. "You'll find out." She looked at him for a moment longer, then started the big Winnebago and drove away. At the first Seven-11 she pulled in and purchased a pack of Marlboros. Then, before pulling out, she took one out and lit it with a match. The open pack she left on the raised carpeted platform in front of the ashtray, then pocketed the matches.

She was nervous enough to miss a few of the turns even though she had been there once before. She tried to keep her mind on what she had to say, but instead kept slipping into internal debates about whether to go ahead or not. It helped her to think of Eduardo, bound with his fishing tackle and thrown into the Miami River, as well as poor

Mr. Schecter, whose only mistake was that he hated being held prisoner. By the time she arrived she had finished one cigarette and was midway through the second. She pulled to the curb in front of Grimes's office on Alton and turned the ignition off. Then she got the two fluorescent tubes from the back bed and put them on a pillow on the dinette table where they could be seen. She checked that everything was in order, opened the door, and went to see Grimes.

The receptionist had left and the last patient was just departing when Margaret entered the waiting room. She found Grimes alone, straightening up some papers on his desk. It took him a moment to place her, but when he did he stopped with the papers and sat motionless. If he was surprised she wasn't dead yet, his face didn't show it.

"I don't recall your having an appointment," he said slowly.

"This is not a matter of health," Margaret said and remained standing. "It's a matter of . . ." she paused and looked around the office, ". . . a matter of money."

"That's odd," he replied. "Why do you think I'd be interested in your finances?" He leaned back and withdrew a cigarette from a pack on his desk and lit it. "Unless, of course, it has something to do with your ability to pay my bill."

"On the contrary, Doctor Grimes, it has something to do with your ability to recover the drugs Forstman hid." She watched his face. "Which I have now acquired."

His expression didn't change. "What drugs are we talking about, Mrs. . . ."

"Binton," she helped him. "We are talking about that last shipment of uncut cocaine that your friends hid, probably on your instructions. We're talking about two fluorescent bulbs on the top floor of Forstman's Rest Home loaded with the stuff." She smiled politely. "That's what drugs we're talking about."

This time his expression did change, even though he tried to control it. Starting at his neck, a suffusion of color crept upward until his face turned a shade lighter than cheap rosé wine. His eyes squinted as though he had been hit with light from an unexpected source. He took another puff and said, "I see. And you've told the police."

"Not yet."

"And why is that?" Grimes asked.

"Well, quite frankly it was totally unexpected. Call it a lucky guess. One minute I'm looking to scrape up enough money to get out of this state and go back home, the next I've got what could be several hundred thousand dollars falling into my lap. But I have a problem." Margaret continued. "You may have a way of disposing of it. To me it's just a lot of useless powder. I don't have the uh, resources or contacts that you might have . . . if you see what I mean."

"Where do you have it?"

Margaret waved the question away. "First, let's get to the heart of the matter."

Grimes attempted a smile but it came out somewhat mangled. "Which is?"

"Which is that I'm willing to give you both light tubes, you can check them if you want, after which I'll disappear. Just a simple exchange. I give you the cocaine, you give me two hundred thousand dollars in cash." She adjusted the lapel on her dress. "After all, my Social Security checks don't nearly cover my expenses in New York. Such an expensive city, don't you know."

Grimes crushed the cigarette out in his ashtray and looked back up at her. He studied her, and as he did the forced smile evened out and was followed by a gruff little laugh. "And all the time I thought you were working for some private investigator or the police. Who set you up for this?"

"Doctor Grimes, this is strictly free-lance. I figured it all out on my own and now it's time to cash in. Two hundred thousand is a cheap price for what I'm offering." She took a step closer. "So, do we have a deal?"

"Two hundred thousand in cash just like that. You must think I have a thick mattress."

"I'll give you a day to get it. I'm not unreasonable."

Grimes kept his eyes on her innocent face framed by an even more innocent hairdo that ended in a neat bun on the top of her head. He stayed that way, without moving, for at least a minute, then spoke.

"How about a hundred and we call it even. A hundred grand, lady, is more than you'll ever see in a church bingo pot."

"Doctor Grimes, it seems to me I'm the one that should be coming out with those cute remarks, not you. It's two hundred thousand or nothing. You know you're going to do it, so stop messing around. It's late."

He put his hand on the phone and pulled it a few inches closer. "I could call the police and tell them about your little offer right now. I'm a respected member of the medical community here in Miami. They'd believe every word I said."

"You could," she replied, "but you won't." She glared at him and waited. If he was good at playing poker, he had misplayed his hand this time. Margaret was not about to be bluffed. "Come on," she said after neither of them had moved for another half minute, "tell me it's a deal, and I'll show you the stuff right away."

He exhaled and nodded slowly. "Okay, it's a deal," he said. "But only if it's the right stuff."

"Of course it's the right stuff," she said. "You think I want to wind up at the bottom of the Miami River?"

He shot her a quick angry glance and got up.

"Follow me," she said. "It's just outside."

CHAPTER 49

...

Grimes locked the door behind him and followed her outside. It was now fully dark and few people were moving along Alton. She walked next to him, then motioned for them to turn a corner. The van was parked twenty feet down the side street.

As soon as Grimes saw the Winnebago he stopped. Margaret turned around and motioned for him to continue.

"You got it in there?" he asked and Margaret noticed a new tone of nervousness in his voice.

"Yeah. Let me just unlock it."

"Bring it out here," Grimes said but Margaret shook her head.

"My terms," she said. "You think I'm crazy enough to bring it outside? You want to see the stuff, you come inside." She took the keys out and opened the side door. Then she stepped up into the van and turned on the overhead lights. She threw the ignition and door keys onto the table next to the light tubes. "You coming?" she called, and shortly thereafter, Grimes took the first step up. When he saw the fluorescent lights displayed he must have felt less anxiety, because he closed the door after him and came up the rest of the way.

"I think you'll recognize these," she said. "They're the only fluorescent light bulbs in the world with screw-off caps." She picked one up and started unscrewing the end. She removed it and held it up for Grimes to look inside. He put two fingers down and, in a pincer movement, withdrew the first plastic bag, rolled into a tight cylinder. He put it on

212

the table next to her keys and stuck a finger inside. After touching it to his tongue, he closed the bag and then up-ended the tube on the table. Slowly, and after he did some shaking, six more bags tumbled out. He repeated the same procedure with each bag, then repacked everything back inside the tube.

"First one seems to be okay," he said matter of factly. "How about the second one?"

Margaret moved it closer and as she did, took a step to the side.

"Don't you think it's hot in here?" she said. "This may take some time. I think I'll put on the generator to get some air-conditioning."

It took him less than a second to register her comment, and when he did he put out a hand and grabbed her arm.

"No." His face looked pale. "No air-conditioning." He frowned and pulled her a little closer.

"But it's so stuffy. How about the exhaust fan?"

He thought for a moment then nodded. "Okay. Just no generator." He turned back to the last fluorescent tube and started in on it. Margaret switched the fan on and imme-diately its steady hum filled the inside of the van. She moved closer to the side door and bent down to look out-side through its top glass panel. It didn't take her long to spot her three friends coming out from the background shadows of a nearby building in response to her signal. She turned back toward Grimes and waited.

After another three minutes he repacked the second tube and put it together with the first on the pillow. When he slowly turned back toward Margaret there was not even a pretense of a smile on his face. Rather, he looked as if he had just come to an unpleasant decision. He looked straight at her and said, "What makes you think I can't just walk right out with the stuff."

"I guess you haven't looked outside." Margaret nodded in the direction of the door and her three friends. "Oh, did I forget to mention that I have some partners in this deal?" She leaned on a cabinet next to her. "The last thing they'd like to see is you leaving without my permission. I might add that Sidney, the gentleman that Franco tried to kill, has a particularly nasty habit of holding grudges and would love an opportunity to even things up. He's the taller gentleman with his hand in his pocket. I'm not sure what's inside but I think it's quite hard." She smiled again and moved a step closer. "Honestly, Doctor Grimes. I don't understand you. It's only two hundred thousand. Why play games?"

Grimes's eyes darted first to the little group outside the front door, then back to the fluorescent light tubes next to him. Slowly his eyes shifted an inch closer to where Margaret's keys were. His hand went casually into his pocket and he cleared his throat. "I don't believe he has anything. I think you're just a bunch of old farts barely keeping one step ahead of senility. Maybe this is your idea of excitement, but I think you've made a serious miscalculation."

"Do you now?" Margaret said, and remained motionless.

Grimes removed his hand and in it was a bright stainless steel tool. It was obviously used in some surgical procedure because one end had a very sharp hooked edge, and the side of it had several serrated teeth. Margaret backed up a step involuntarily and felt her heel go over the edge of the stepdown to the door. She reached out to steady herself, but Doctor Grimes took the job away from her. He grabbed her by her other arm and forced her down into the door well. The hand with the tool came up and cut her dress over her shoulder on its way toward her neck. One or two little drops of blood seeped out and added color to the black and white printed pattern. He held the tool at her jugular, and then said in a voice full of rage, "Open the door."

Margaret felt for the handle with her hand and when she found it, pushed down. The door swung out and she saw three pairs of shocked eyes staring at her and the scalpel-like tool at her throat. She didn't even have time to swallow. Grimes gave her a forceful shove in the small of her back and she went flying out the door. She glanced off Durso, then her knee hit the curb and she grimaced with pain. Fortunately her shoulder hit a little green patch of grass along the edge of the street. Before she had a chance to turn over and catch her breath, Grimes had the door reclosed and locked. Not long after that the big Winnebago motor turned over with a roar.

"My God," Berdie screamed. "He's killed her." She was on her knees next to her friend and looking at the red stain on Margaret's sleeve.

"I don't think so," Sid said, "But he's shaken her up a lot." He placed his hand under her neck and raised her to a sitting position. Margaret winced as her leg straightened, and grabbed the nearest arm.

"I need a moment," she said. She breathed deeply, then looked at the anxious faces around her. "It's my knee. I think I'll need some help standing."

"Relax," Durso said. "Where do you think you're going? That son of a bitch just drove off in our Winnebago."

Margaret nodded. "I thought he would if given half the chance." She rubbed the knee slowly and tried flexing it a little. After a moment, she assured herself it wasn't broken. "Bruised knee and a scratch on the arm is a cheap enough price," she said.

Sid frowned. "Price? For what?"

The explosion took them by surprise. It was not on the block, but it was close enough to crack every window in the house behind them. The four of them turned in the direction of the loud noise and saw from around the corner on Alton the reddish flare of fire from something burning. They couldn't see what it was, but Margaret assured them that it was their van. Within moments people were pouring out of their houses and shops and running around the corner to the accident. Margaret leaned on Durso's and Sid's arms, and pulled herself to a standing position.

"What the hell happened?" Durso said.

"It was his own bomb," Margaret said dully, almost as though she was convincing herself of something. "He put it there and wired it to kill us. I had to be sure it was his." She looked at her friends. "It was. He was scared of the auxiliary generator."

"So why in God's name would he turn the switch?" Berdie asked.

"Oh, he didn't," Margaret said and took a tentative step. Her knee was tightening up but she could still put a little weight on it. "That was the last thing he was about to do. He just wanted to get away and grab the cocaine."

"So, what did he do?" Sid asked.

"Well, if you were a smoker like I am, you wouldn't have to ask. Remember, he was in a very excited state. He simply took one of the Marlboros I left for him . . . his own brand. And because he was driving and in a hurry to get away, and since I didn't leave him any matches"—she looked at the others without expression—"he used the dashboard lighter."

The flames were now getting high enough so that they could see the top of them above a two-story building. A column of smoke coiled up into the night sky. The distant noise of a siren could be heard coming from somewhere around the South Beach.

"But . . ." Berdie began, "the lighter?"

"A little rewiring from Renan Alvarez," Margaret added, "a favor for the sake of an old friend." They watched for a few minutes more in silence until the sirens grew unbearably loud and passed on Alton.

"Well, so much for the van," Durso said wistfully.

"There you go being pessimistic again," Sid scoffed. "Think positive, think of the insurance money."

Margaret turned away.

"Grimes was right, you know." A little mischievous smile played across her face and was just barely visible in the light from the flames. "He said that cigarettes would kill him, and they did."